The wind had b... dress above my knees, revealing the full and tempting roundness of my thighs. This did the trick! George's eyes portrayed repressed emotions; his extremely nervous hands bespoke his inward desires most profoundly.

He placed the rug at my feet and drew it upward very slowly. When he had reached my dimpled knees he paused, then placed his hands between them. He did this so artfully that if I hadn't guessed otherwise I would have sworn it was an accident. With his hands still between my knees he continued to draw the rug upward, thus deliberately uncovering my legs as he went. I hoped he wouldn't stop because that day I wore no panties. . .

ANONYMOUS

FLOSSIE
The Memoirs of a
Jazz Baby

A STAR BOOK

published by
the Paperback Division of
W. H. Allen & Co. PLC

A Star Book
Published in 1986
by the Paperback Division of
W. H. Allen & Co. PLC
44 Hill Street, London W1X 8LB

Printed in Great Britain by
Anchor Brendon Ltd, Tiptree, Essex

ISBN 0 352 318554

❦ 1 ❧

1

I was spending the day window shopping.
As I gazed into a window in which I saw
displayed pretty lace lingerie and exquisite
open-work stockings, all on seductively
shaped forms, I suddenly became aware of
someone at my side, who no doubt was
appraising my girlish contours. His eyes
bespoke a man who might be thinking: "Boy
I'll bet she'd make a good fuck! Could I go
for her? Think I'll try to make her." What
else could he be thinking about? Yes, what
could the thoughts of a man be who tries to
pierce the filmy costume and the scanty
undies which a daring young miss wears on
a warm summer day.

This person sauntered a step here and a
step there, running his eyes up and down
my shapely calves perhaps trying to imagine
what they looked like above my dress, and
exactly how I was formed where my legs
met.

Modesty, I continued to act as though I
wasn't being noticed, but soon I found that

I had difficulty in controlling my curiosity. I wanted to know exactly what my new admirer looked like. By slyly glancing through the corners of my eyes I discerned that he was a quite handsome man of middle age. He was still feasting gluttonously on my well-shaped legs, which were garbed in black silk stockings so sheer that the milky whiteness of my virgin calves gleamed through most alluringly. My gown, which was made with as little material as was possible to cover the female form within the law, moulded so clingingly to my figure that it wantonly revealed the tempting fullness and sensuously rounded contours of my pliant, maiden torso. Of course, the greatest attraction—my very definitely defined bosom—pointed out teasingly and challengingly. The nipples daringly nosed their way forward and saucily danced at every step I made. My long golden curls flirted with a moderate breeze; some caressed my freely exposed shoulders while others pranced about my large irresistible blue eyes, tickling my nose and stringing in the folds of my meshy cupid's-bow lips. This refreshing zephyr often caught the hem of my skirt and raised it far above my knees, revealing my pink laced panties, and the charming nudity of my thighs; it also blew my skirt deep into the crevice of my plump, round bottom.

As a whole, I formed the kind of picture that made men say: "I want to see more," and that few inches of flabby meat in their pants would suddenly stretch to adult size—at least this man's did, because as I stole another glance I could plainly see his penis bobbing angrily in his pants.

Why I caused this was no mystery to me. In fact, why I attracted most men, particularly this one, who was now so openly and lecherously observing me had been explained to my by my aunt Stella.

I began to feel uncomfortable under my admirer's constant gaze. I sensed that he was measuring and feeling me with his eyes. I felt that his sight had stolen beneath my flimsy attire and was now gloating over the parted mounds of my dainty little white stomach and curly silk blonde hairs that sprouted on either side of my smiling cunnie. I felt a strange warmth tingling in my veins; my shaft became hot, and as this happened he began to falteringly approach me, as if he was trying to frame some appropriate phrase. But instead of speaking to me, which I was certain he would, he edged up close to me and glanced down the dark, well-drawn valley between my creamy white bubbies. My very low-necked dress brazenly exposed the tops of these two delicious marble orbs, but apparently he was not satisfied with this abbreviated view. He tilted his towering head so that out of the slits of his eyes he could get a more satisfying picture of my already hardening mounds. I felt his lust-hungry searching gaze! More dewy moisture trickled out of my yet virgin hole.

I was easily made hot by men, but never before had I ever been aroused, as I was, by merely the "I-want-to-fuck-you" glance of an admiring stranger. Perhaps this was because last night aunt Stella explained to me the full use of the female and male sexual organs. Even while she was telling how to—as she called it—"Straddle a comet," I felt a strong urge arising within me to try it.

Naturally I knew a few things; that is, I was aware of the fact that it was necessary to have something to do with a man in order to get a baby. I knew how to make myself spend. I did this by frantically rubbing my fingers between the two burning, swollen lips of my twat, and also playing with my clitty at the same time. I always thought though, until my aunt righted my illusion, that the man rubbed his prick between the lips as I so often did with my fingers.

Still being "hot in the pants" from last night's lecture I did not puzzle at my condition then. I had been trying to imagine all during my sleepless night and as I walked, how a man's rigid love lance would feel deeply buried in my itching coozie. In fact, with every man that passed I tried to imagine exactly what the thing between his legs looked like, and I continued repeating to myself, "I wonder how he would feel in me?"

Since I knew exactly what was on this man's mind, who was now alternating his eyes from me to the scanties in the window, I flushed with the rich pigment of a very embarrassed, modest girl. But was it a blush caused by modesty or was it a token of expression worn by a girl who felt that her lustful cravings were being successfully read by this fascinating stranger?

The ardent and the admiring way he examined me was flattering not because of his attention, but because his general appearance suggested a man who was not only a leader of his kind but also a possessor of amorous skill and physical attractiveness.

Moving still closer to my side, my admirer tipped his hat artfully and in a genial, low, but steady voice said: "Pardon me, but evidently we have something in common."

I looked up, hardly daring to speak, because the magnetic charm in his voice seemed to trickle right through my ears down to my already burning slit, and increase the strength of my throbbings there. I did summon enough aplomb to coolly, but shyly, say: "I don't understand. . . ."

"We both seem to admire pretty things," he broke in, "like these dainty thin hose, and little flesh-tinted, filmy underwear."

"Oh, I do," I exclaimed expectantly. "I just adore such things!"

"Well," he continued, "you are an unusually charming and pretty girl. Surely you would look many times as tempting in those petite silken undies than you do now."

I felt offended, but my scorn melted as I scrutinized this hypnotic-voiced person thoroughly for the first time. I saw a very distinguished looking, elderly gentleman, with handsome streaks of silver running through a well groomed, once raven, crop of hair.

His dress and mannerisms revealed a man of wealth and culture. The twinkle in his sparkling, well-set, jet eyes reflected a jocose and witty alertness. The general shape of his head betrayed a person of intellect and power. The upper lip of his passion-sensitive mouth was adorned with a neatly trimmed moustache. His chin confirmed the story his lips spoke; it bore the imprint of a sensuous nature.

He had merely attracted me when I observed him at first but now, since I had studied him more carefully, he fascinated me. Warm magnetic waves swept through my body and my pulse beat faster, as this seemingly perfect representative of the prick-bearing sex nudged still closer to get an even more complete view of my already hard-nippled bubbies. Perhaps he was trying to see if his vision would carry him down to my moss-covered mound?

Blush? Why shouldn't I? It seemed like my throbbing vent was now emitting enough moisture to be seen dripping down on the inner sides of my shapely thighs. At least it felt that way to me. Yes, I blushed like a crimson rose; the mirrored walls in the shop window proved this more definitely to me. Oh, I could always blush when the occasion warranted it; that was one of my feminine assets.

Again he spoke, slowly, as if he was trying to strike a happy medium for congenial conversation: "My dear child, don't you think that one of your age is slightly too young to be thinking of buying such feminine adornments? Why more mature ladies usually wear those ... well ... er ... to make themselves more seductively enticing," he finished, anxious not to be offensive.

"Oh pshaw! No!" I replied, shaking my curls and glancing at him mischievously. "Girls are never too young to dress prettily, that is to try to tempt men—certain men," I finished insinuatingly, and by the inviting look in my eyes I had hoped he would have been able to tell that he was one of those certain men.

We chatted for a few moments. I laid a net of verbal enticement before him. Satisfied that he could fuck me in the proper surroundings he at length bowed curtly and introduced himself; at the same time he handed me his card. It read:

SHIPBUILDER

I suppressed a cry of delight! A man of wealth, power and perhaps a connoisseur of women, used to only the best, had gone out of his way to speak to me, a girl far beneath his social strata. I felt that he was the man who was destined to take my cherry! I shamelessly wished that it would be that way.

When he invited me to lunch I was both surprised, because I thought he would overlook me on account of my class, and embarrassed. I was not properly attired to lunch with him. He finally persuaded me to go by saying:

"Your piquant youth, your refreshing, humble beauty, your love-inspiring figure, and your agreeable manner are quite enough to afford you a rousing welcome at Rector's."

This famous restaurant was a rendezvous for the youths, beauties, and the sports of the town. It was my first experience in a place as glamorous as that. I was amazed at the wanton display of feminine charms, yet I was consoled, because I did the same. Profanity and immoralty seemed the vogue there.

My friend was most lavish with his courtesy—he dazzled me with flattery. Not once did he remove his lust-hungry eyes from me. Twice he purposely dropped his handkerchief so that he could feast his blazing eyes on my appetizing, denuded thighs. The second time this occurred I purposely drew my dress clear up to my lace, transparent panties, and I spread my legs apart. My! I almost swooned, I was so tantalized by that burning-tingling-itching blood in my hot, prick-hungry, immaculate box. That is, I could really feel his eyes touch my clitoris, or it was some strong ray that emitted from them when he focused his vision, oh, so longingly—I could tell—on my swollen-lipped hungry cunnie mouth. I had a very hard time trying to prevent myself from putting my hand firmly over the burning slit, but somehow I did escape. I moved about impetuously in my seat, opening and closing my legs, trying to force myself to come. This inward excitement must have made me look prettier because Roland spoke:

"Flossie, my dear lovely girl, your sweet little rosebud mouth was made to be kissed, and the petite girlish charms that you so innocently exposed and allowed me to gaze upon were created and fashioned for the heavenly enjoyment of some appreciative lover. You are tempting! You are maddening!" Apparently he was in the grip of an overwhelming hard-on, then he continued with more aplomb: "Your shapely legs, your thighs, your dreamy Venus-like orbs—" he paused to catch his breath—"Flossie, I have seen hundreds of girls in my days, a lot of them with shapely legs, attractive torsos, but I swear, dear Flossie, none of them were so ravishingly desirable. Oh, if only I could say what I feel! I could eat you! Your figure! Your face! All of you . . . a tempting, luscious irresistible bon-bon!"

There was a ring of real sincerity in his extravagant compliments. I was afraid at first that what he had begun to say would be just more honey-coated flattery, but as he spoke I could see that he was becoming more serious all along. Yes, he meant every syllable of his vow-like speech.

I was careful not to indulge too unwisely and too freely in the tempting, strong drinks. I did not wish to injure the very favourable impression that I had made on Roland, but I had taken enough to set my hot blood afire. That tormenting itch in my sympathetic pussy continued to burn even more hotly. Very little stimulation was ever needed to make me steam.

Roland must have read my mood:

"Come, my little bon-bon," he said play-boyishly, "let us go to the park. A ride will do you good. You will be revived and your nerves will be soothed."

What a fool I must have been to try to conceal my real feelings at that time. I was trembling hot. I needed a big, fat, juicy, stiff prick between my legs more badly than anything in the world. I wanted to cultivate a more intimate acquaintance with this enrapturing bon vivant to accomplish that purpose. Hadn't I felt my nectar dripping from my angrily throbbing womb ever since I met him? And wasn't I in the market for a good time? And hadn't I been dreaming ever since last night how wonderful it might be to have a thick, beating, male monster shoved way up into my uterus? And wasn't I always trying to improve my education? Then what in the deuce was I waiting for? As I said, I must have been a fool.

Because the day was very warm, Roland had procured a touring car, and a chauffeur to drive. I was deeply distressed, because I knew that it would be impossible to extinguish the devilish heat in my box in a car of ths type. I could accomplish very little with a driver in the front seat.

As we rode through the tree-lined mall of the park a feeling of boldness crept into my system. Hang the pedestrians and to hell with the chauffeur, I thought. My pussy was hot and I wanted to get it plugged. If my desire would have driven me mad, I reasoned, would that have been better than to let a few people witness the fucking scene, which I so badly ached for? Was it less desirable to be driven mad by a blood-shot cunnie? Or was it a greater evil to be exposed in the midst of a soul saving, so-much-dreamed-of, sexual act? It was a perplexing problem, but I decided in favour of my lust-seeking maiden cunnie.

I nestled closer to him and then I threw my legs carelessly across the top of a half-unfolded auxiliary seat. The wind rushed in and soothingly caressed me beneath my dress; the place where I felt my entire attention drawn to became somewhat eased. I wantonly moved my thighs a bit more apart to allow the breeze to more freely lick my seething vent. This uncovered my thighs many times and exposed them clearly, to my silk-covered, smouldering box. As though I had been embarrassed, I quickly recovered my denuded parts, each time making some playful and teasing remark. I could tell that I was making progress because of his many short gasps of both surprise and delight. I could sense his steady licentious gaze glutting over the shapeliness of my feminine charms.

We nibbled on everything in general for conversation. After we had disposed of a great deal of this kind of half-interesting chatter, he sat up and looked into my eyes:

"By jove, dear Flossie, never before have I seen such seductiveness in any one pair of legs. What an exquisite form you have. I can almost picture your nude form silhouetted in the rays of the moon. I would give you a hundred dollars to see you nude!" he spurted

18

impulsively, then after pausing for a reaction, he continued, "Can I tempt you with the offer?"

Gee! Wasn't that a bold beginning? I thought. I was delighted, and amazed too, at his making such a daring offer after so short an acquaintance. At the same time, as I prepared myself to answer him, I let my elbow rest in his lap and with apparent innocence allowed it to press down upon his hidden, bursting monster. It felt like one. (I even wondered how a woman could get a thing as big as that in her hole. I knew I even had a difficult time last night in getting my finger in!)

"Why, Roland!" I pretended, modestly, "don't you think you are going a little too far by asking me to undress so soon? You know our acquaintance is very recent," I paused for a few minutes; I wanted him to gain the impression that I was thinking. Then turning my head saucily away, I continued, "Haven't I shown you enough already?" Then I swung my head back to glance at him with a sly, bewitching sparkle in my eyes and puckered my lips poutingly.

It so happened at the time I finished that we were passing through a secluded, thickly-wooded cove in the park. Roland seemed fully aware of this protection. In a flash he had me twined in his strong, but gentle arms, and his lips found mine. He pressed my mouth more firmly to his as the time passed.

I almost swooned from the effects of this hot, absorbing, pussy-tickling kiss.

Too weakened by the intoxicating aftermath of the first burning caress, I submissively yielded to another amorous attack. His lips were resilient but firm. His soft, silky, and adorable moustache tickled my face and added to the sensual feeling.

We parted for a few seconds to gaze mutely and dreamingly into each other's eyes. Then he clasped me to him again, this time though, he clamped his hand firmly over my left bubbie—gee! What a torrid gust of passion shook my frame. I felt my sensitive pussy shiver with delight. Not satisfied with my reaction to his attack, he again found my lips with his. I was so lust maddened by this time that I dared anything. With his tongue he pried my lips apart, a favour that I dearly appreciated, and into my mouth he shot his flaming love dagger, and swabbed the walls with his inciting flesh. Boy, did I vibrate! I could feel my red-hot blood racing through my eyes. I was so damn hot I couldn't even moan! My cunt was so scalding that I was paralyzed by the intense delicious heat there. Oh, why didn't a big prick enter and end my devilish misery?

The violent frenzied movements of his arms and the quivering of his lips, as they sucked and chewed mine, also revealed very plainly his passion-intoxicated condition.

Since the ice was broken, I yielded to his

every advance and even induced him onward, that is, as much as our short acquaintance would allow.

I slipped my tongue into his mouth and there our two molten daggers welded together I shook even more violently in his arms. He drew a long breath and then added pressure to his hand which was still greedily fingering my heaving bubbies. They protruded plainly through my thin, silk waist.

"Oh, Roland," I gasped, "what a perfect lover you are."

"And, Flossie, dearest," he returned with more control, "what a perfect inspiration you are."

Then we folded into another lingering, soul-scorching kiss.

He bathed and nipped my lips with his; so cunt teasingly, yet so soothingly. His hand stealthily began to creep up my thigh. The sensitive skin there tried to writhe from his feverish touch, but that magnetic intangible something, which the masculine hand near the female nest produces, would not allow me to worm from his, make-you-want-to-fuck, nestling hand. Instead my cunnie involuntarily moved down to meet its approaching visitor. My plump little bottom was bouncing around in agonizing pleasure. Then I clutched his hand as we broke from another embrace.

"Oh, Roland! Please, oh! Please! Don't

Roland!" I panted in my cunt-itching delirium. Try as I might, I shall never forgive myself for saying that. What made me say it? I don't know.

"But . . ." he mumbled as though he wanted to say something and changed his mind. His progress stopped.

"Roland, dear, this is neither the time nor the place for real loving, is it?"

"Well, no, not a very comfortable place," he half-heartedly agreed.

"Dear, I think you are the most charming man—you are. You are making me forget myself. I really object to your advances." I guess, while I said this, if my pussy had the power it would shoot me for not wanting to end its torture immediately. "Gee, I hardly even know you!"

"That may be true Flossie, but . . . take my word for it! Somehow, I can't get the idea into my head that I met you only a few hours ago. I feel like I've known you all my life. Perhaps it's because all my life I've dreamed of meeting a girl like you." As he spoke, his manner brewed into sincere sentimentality.

'To tell you the truth, Roland, dear, I feel the same way. You seem fascinating. Your voice, you—oh, I don't know how to say it. When I look at you, I hear you talk, you touch me with your hand, everything about you makes me ache all over for you. You send warm lustful currents through my whole body."

"Flossie," he said, as he patted and fumbled my shaking hand, "we will get better acquainted in the future. Tomorrow, if you find you are able, I want you to meet me at the ferry in Jersey. I shall have one of my own cars, a town limousine, and a chauffeur—you know, the see nothing, hear nothing type.

"We will take a long ride through the Jersey countryside and then dine at the Palais D'Coite. It is a place noted for its excellent cuisine. They specialize in the preparation of foods promoting love's lotions. All the sporting parties meet there because of the privacy they offer. Of course you'll join me," he looked at me pleadingly, "won't you, Flossie?"

I answered him by nestling in his arms, mine entwined his neck. I was always able to do this act with alluring seductiveness, and I kissed him with every bit of unrefined animal passion that I had in my tongue— which in this case spoke for my whole cunt-burning soul.

"Roland, of course I'll be there, I can hardly wait. I know we'll have such a wonderful time."

He then took me to my train, and after repeating my promise to meet him we parted, ending a day eventful with scorching lascivious wants. These, incidentally, still remained within me unabated. Could I wait for the approaching day, or would I go mad with my desires?

❧ 2 ❧

2

When I reached home, which I shall always call Aunt Stella's Bohemian apartment, I was anxiously greeted by my only relative. Aunty wasn't, as that title suggests, old maidish and conservative. She was a woman generously supplied with charms—that is, she had a coozie that was wedged between two shapely plump thighs and which I think was as anxious for big-pricked visitors, as I had now begun to be. Many were the nights when I found comfort and solace by burying my disappointed lust-seeking face between the vales of her two generous, yet symmetrical titties. Oh, how I used to love to suck and fondle these two enticing lumps of creamy-white flesh! And how beautiful she looked in her passionate ecstasy as I used to perform this oh, so cherishing and exciting feat; how nice and rubbery they used to taste.

Stella was only thirty-three, but her face erased more than eight years from her actual age. Her actions and frivolous sexual attitude were all so carefree, comparable to the shaking of her dimpled meaty bottom as she walked. Men oftentimes followed her for miles attempting to either gain her favour or else determine where such a fuckable mass of human flesh might live. This I knew to be a fact.

She was a contrast to me in the colour of her hair and skin. Her eyes were the jewel-black passionate kind. She played the role of girl friend, rather than that of kin.

Stella noticed the new light in my eyes. Naturally I must have looked different for hadn't I had a glimpse into a more cunt-full and prick-full life? She exclaimed:

"Hi, hon. My, but you're late. Where—oh, oh, now what have you been up to? Come tell your little auntie the cause of that shining look in your eyes. You have the same kind of sparkle in them that Sarah had the first night her husband put his delicious six shooter in, by the way, how I KNOW it was delicious."

"Now, auntie dear, what are you trying to accuse me of?"

"How did you like it? Wasn't it the grandest feeling. It makes me hot just to think about it."

"But honestly, Stell, I don't quite get you." I pretended innocently.

She neared me, then without warning she playfully unbalanced me and I fell upon the soft pillow padded floor. She picked up my dress and removed my panties, before I could recover from the shock.

"Quit it, Stell. What's the matter?"

"I won't, you sly little dear, not until I get the truth and your pussy's mouth is going to speak it. I kind of thought you would go and do it today. You wouldn't let me sleep last night. You had your legs twined around my bottom all last night, and you should have seen the way you were rolling that can of yours. Why I had to reach for my faithful dildo three times—naughty girl. You lesbian! Now spread your legs . . . wide!"

Her actions and speech had renewed the heat in my box, so I found it a pleasure to obey her mother-like command.

"You are disgusting," she continued, as she opened my lips real wide and kissed my inflamed and swollen cunnie. "Ah but . . . mmm, your panties are all soiled, now young lady how did that happen?"

Dear Aunt Stell, she seemed to understand me so perfectly. I couldn't resist confessing to her the events of the day.

"And you didn't fuck him yet?" she asked, after I finished telling of my clitty raising experience.

"But, Stell, I hardly know him," I argued, modestly.

"And you'll never know him any better unless you let him stretch that cute little twat of yours."

"Do you really mean that?"

29

"You poor little fool, what in the hell do you think a twat was made for . . . glory? Or the worms? Look at your poor little hole; see how swollen and hot it is."

"Now quit ribbing me so much. My little cunnie is hurting me enough as it is."

I waited all night for the dawn to break. I was too peter-thirsty to go to sleep. I didn't want to make myself spend. I wanted to save every drop of my luscious love dew for the ever approaching moment when I would be gigantically thrilled by that cream-spurting meat stick of Roland's; swabbing every cell of sensitive rubbery flesh in my vaginal folds.

I arose about nine o'clock in the morning. Nervous anxiety thundered in my chest, for I was still parched for that juicy meat in Roland's pants.

I clothed myself in an envelope chemise of diaphanous silk. Drawers would have been a hindrance, so I did not put them on. I rolled my sheer black stockings low enough to expose the dimples of my baby-skin knees.

Over all this I wore a flimsy dress with a mild tinting of pink. This plain-cut outfit clung to my form in a skin-on-a-grape fashion. My well exposed bust gleamed and even sparkled with my virgin freshness. The clothed part of my dancing bubbies protruded saucily and provokingly.

The skirt of my dress hung as if glued to my gracefully swaying, polished round ass.

The dimples on either flank were deliciously moulded; in fact, I made a picture of what one might call "The Pinnacle of Feminine Seductiveness."

As I dared not walk in the street, exposed as I was, I put on an overall of white linen. This coat reached almost to my ankles. It dutifully covered my liberally displayed legs and immaculate apparel. I wore a white tam to blend with the wrap.

After being kissed and wished good luck by my aunt I left the house.

On the way to the ferry, Roland was conjured to my mind! I tried to imagine how his nutritious meat loaf looked, how big it was. And when I tried to imagine how this luscious piece of human, cunt-seeking meat would behave in my unused eager slit, again I felt that tingling-melting sensation in my sweetly perfumed love nest. There was an instant when I even feared that his divine rod might not contain the vigour of the average male; perhaps this was because I judged him to be past forty. While that tinge of morbidity stained my thoughts, I also imagined that his unsated prick might be the worse, and impaired from wear.

Roland had arrived at the appointed place as I entered upon the scene. Apparently he didn't recognize me, dressed as I was, in the chic tam and long coat. He looked about carefully, his eyes rested on me, then his face reflected bitter disappointment. I wanted to see how badly he really wanted me, a scheme impelled by feminine vanity, so I decided to remain incognito and observe his actions.

After watching him grow to the point of acute anxiety I walked over to him and spoke:

"Well, Roland, you don't seem to remember me, do you?"

He demuringly examined me with a wry face.

"Now, Roland, you naughty boy, you have a surprise coming." I spoke in an unchaste, coy manner, as I hopped into the car in which he was sitting. I raised my bottom so that I could free myself from the long coat and I also discarded the tam. By doing this I revealed the undisguised and tempting Flossie.

He gasped in surprised delight as his eyes in one glance devoured all of my seductiveness.

"Egad, little girl, you are a dream!"

I could plainly see his rising pants-shielded cunt-lollypop. His face glowed and beamed. He was already imagining his approaching carnal meal. And what a meal it was going to be! I hoped so.

He reached for me just as the chauffeur geared the car, but the sudden jerking of the vehicle aided him; it threw me right into his arms.

I too began to notice the clothes he wore. He had on an immaculately pressed white

Palm Beach, a very appropriate suit for that warm day. His genuine under-water-woven panama lay on the seat next to him. His hair was carefully groomed. His skin reflected the freshness of youth. I assumed that he was the type who lived by the rules of scrupulous cleanliness and neatness; he would exact the same from his companions.

The automobile in which we were riding was of the town-car type, with a private cabin for the driver. Our cabin was luxuriously equipped with comforts. By raising the auxiliary seats a bed could be made . . . not any less comfortable than mine at home. In fact, we even had one more advantage than the average hotel room, the soothing breeze flowing through, caused by the moving car.

I remained on his lap just long enough to receive a short but twat-burning kiss. He tried to touch my bare knee. I repulsed him, not because I didn't want him to do this, but for one very good reason: I knew that I could not stand much more of his clitty-exciting treatment. I would become so blinded by it that I would give in to my screaming-for-screw swollen lipped cunnie and bring shame on both of us, by pulling his staff out of his pants and shoving it all the way up into my quivering oval belly. Therefore I remarked:

"Roland, dear, you must put the shades down if you wish to take such liberties."

At once he acted upon my suggestion. Even the chauffeur couldn't see us after he had completed this task. It was now so comfortable, secluded and nestlike; even nature couldn't have offered a more appropriate trysting place. At last the stage was set!

I hastily threw my arms about his neck and sought his mouth with my poised lips. How wonderful and thrilling that kiss was! I caressed him, wildly tonguing and lipping his fire emitting mouth. By this fierce and soul-stirring attack I tried to suggest to him what could be expected if he properly directed his erotic talents.

Between body-inflamed kisses, as we rode, Roland outlined a brief history of his life. He had been married once and as a result he had a son who was now twenty-two. He lived in the sporting centre of the Occidental World, Paris. His wife died while giving birth. His boy was at this time managing his European industries. From the way he spoke about his son I judged that he loved him very dearly. The conversation then drifted to matters such as his analysing his personality and other confidential topics. All this, I realized, was done by him to make me trust him implicitly as well as to increase my longing and lustful desire. If he had noticed my very suggestive attitude, or had he even tried to pierce my flimsy gown and saw that

I wore no drawers on this occasion, he would have known that I would have been an easy sacrifice on the altar of Venus. His romantic phrases and his soft, full voice had almost as much effect upon my pussy as his coddling hands.

"Now, Flossie," he continued after outlining his character and his attitude towards morals, etc., "I want you to know exactly how I feel about you . . . and my strongly passionate nature.

"All my life I have been, you might say, a ladies' man. I am very fond of feminine charms and the soulful bliss they afford me. In fact, I am a very discriminating sensualist, meaning of course, that I have an abnormal lustful appetite. My particular appetite craves girls of your age and type. I like your charms, that baby-like softness, yet tender firmness and vigour. Angelic innocence such as you alone possess is so deliciously satisfying to a man of my nature and age.

"I have had intercourse and have indulged in every type of passion's embraces with every kind of female loveliness." He paused to moisten his lips, like a dog who thinks about the swell bone he just had, then continued. "I can truthfully say, Flossie dear, that I have never met a girl as desirable as you." He finished gloating over my half-concealed titties and my partially exposed robust thighs.

"You, every bit of you, suggests to me, you dainty little devil . . ." he nipped my cheek, "such sensual delghts—so deliciously seductive.

"You are intelligent, I presume, well read and very conscious of your bewitching charms, but somehow you seem to display the pureness and innocence of a child. It makes you so much more . . . I can't explain!" He quivered and squeezed his bursting prick in his hand. He was almost overcome with emotion.

Suddenly he released his apparently giant stiff from his hand and made a wild, but successful lunge at me. He drew me so firmly to his breast that I shuddered in delightful pain. A fire had shot from the tips of my rock-hard titties down into my palpitating peter-wanter. He drew my head down to his broad bosom; I was hot! But this was only a mild beginning, as I afterwards found out.

I tilted my imprisoned head upwards and looked into his eyes with a glance that was bedimmed by a filmy coat of passion's moisture. I was dazed by my inflaming needs. Even my lips, which were sopped by the excessive salivation of my mouth, quivered, screaming my inward cuntful emotions. Then—oh it was so glorious—he poured an avalanche of sensuous kisses upon my awaiting lips. He did this tenderly and effectively; at the same time he sucked and chewed, oh so deliciously, upon this outpost of my pussy telegraph system. He laid his free hand over my waiting milky orbs. First he played with these through the thin covering of my semi-transparent waist and then he fondled them after they bounced out of their very inefficient hiding place. Each time he rubbed my cute little nipples with his warm and hypnotic fingers a more rabid wave of wanting-to-make-me-fuck emotion shook my prick-greedy frame.

Oh, how I longed for something between my lust-sweated and cunt-dewed thighs! How I squeezed my legs together, and how I wormed and wiggled my burning meaty bottom! Yes, that fleshy little spot where my legs come together pined for Roland's visitor. I knew it would slide in and out. I dared not imagine more for fear that I would go mad.

I moved my legs apart, then together, opening and closing my cunnie's mouth! I twisted and moved around like an eel! In my libidinous excitement my dress worked up and exposed me nearly to the waist. My plump, dimpled knees, my round, full thighs were now an added incentive for my lover's searching eyes. His vision even found some of the longer silk hairs of my golden-framed puss.

For a moment he could only pant, he was too paralysed by desire to even speak. I imagined this exposure would produce this reaction. In a trembling voice he gave vent to his feelings:

"Flossie, dear, can I kiss your sweet little legs? God! I never dreamed a woman's legs could be so beautiful, so exciting!"

"Oh, Roland, darling," I panted, "can't you see? I need you! Everything! Everything you have! I am yours. Do what you wish with me! I'm—"

I couldn't finish. The overwhelming heat in my pussy caused by his thorough caressing of my legs with his lips and hands almost choked me with mad desire. From my slender ankle to my mid-thigh he ran his hand, nipping and squeezing as it went along.

"Lord! What exquisite flesh?" he exclaimed while he glided his hand amor-ously and lightly over my smooth, powdered skin.

My cunt, my clitoris, my tits, and my lips, ached more strongly as the time flew for more and greater thrills! If ever there was a woman aflame, it was I. Yet Roland hesi-tated. No doubt he was afraid he might invite some remonstration or incur some resistance. He just didn't know his own power! Nor did he know the state of Flossie's cunt.

Then I said in fluttering words:

"Oh dear, don't stop! Please! Oh, darling, fondle me, everywhere!'

I stretched my legs far apart, praying that he would soon find my helpless slit.

With an expression that was more akin to a moan he uttered:

"I will, darling . . . oh, you angel, I will! At last, at last you are going to be mine."

He shook very noticeably in his anxiety. A virgin was his! He plunged his open hand between my parted legs and clamped it hard up against my pussy's mouth.

"Oh, God," I prayed, "is this heaven?"

I moved my bottom around so that his hand would irritate my lips, but he sensed my desire. He removed my soft silk-curled heated pussy from his hand. With an upward sweep, a delicate and tender finger found my bobbing clitty. No man had ever made me feel that way before! He stroked my legs and thighs, squeezed my full-meated bottom and then—then he almost drove me crazy. He kissed me, beginning at the dimples in my knees, and worked his way up to the perfume-douched cavity of my soul. Would he ever put the real thing in? God, I was dying! I was going blind! I couldn't hear a thing, save the thundering of my heart! My pussy was screaming!

"Put it in! PUT IT IN!"

At last he worked himself between my widely spread legs. I swooned when I saw him pull out a rampant tool from his fallen trousers. Somehow I managed to slip my dress and chemise completely off. He too removed his shorts. I stretched my legs from window to window. I grasped his monster.

I wanted to feel it nude. It almost burned my hand. Gosh, it was hot! It bobbed from my hold!

Everything blurred. I felt my eyes roll wildly in their sockets! Even the lips in my coozie seemed to stretch forward toward their intended visitor. The object of my lustful desires was by this time directly over my seething vent.

"Please! Oh, please! Quick!" I rambled, deliriously.

"I will guide it in, girlie," he said with more reserve.

He parted the curly tuft and opened the tortured mouth of my mellowed cunnie. At last he was astride my moist, burning slit! He pulled me over to him and he slipped forward to get me in a convenient position. God, would he ever put it in? At last! His hand deftly guided his magnificent, but angry, ruby-headed one-eyed tool to my red hot, fleshy, steaming, boiler-like cunt. He worked the head in until it was buried in my tight, puckering, prick-sucking orifice.

"Oh, dearest," I mumbled faintly, "it's going to hurt me dreadfully, I know. I don't care! Oh, ow-woo-oo-oo-oh!"

The first partial insertion thrilled me so, but I held my breath and I grabbed his ass and drew him closer to me. The turgid knob stretched me and slowly began to worm its way into my juicy tube. How my heart fluttered, both from fear of the first cherry-breaking pain and the electrified thrills of this pulsating burning rod.

Little by little it poked its way into my quivering belly. The pain was not as great as I feared it would be. Gosh, oh gee, it was swell!

Roland increased my fires by playing and sucking on my denuded bubbies; he also nipped and plucked my ass. I reacted to this by my cunnie's sucking his prick with harder and ever increasing zeal.

Under the influence of his emotions, Roland swore and cried out in unrestrained, lecherous language. He rose to the heights of obscene eloquence. I was both influenced and delighted by his outcries, perhaps this was because I had never heard such passionate, smutty expressions. I reasoned that Roland would invite an excess of voluptuous outbursts which might emphasize his erotic feelings during the screwing act. I soon accustomed myself to this habit, also, for soon I was wantonly using lewd language to express my feelings as he mustered his big prick in and out of my tickling, itching, flaming hole.

My painfully stretched hole was already beginning to get accustomed to this turgid, monster-cock, which it was struggling to swallow. Now that turgid throbbing mass began to feel so wonderful! It imbued in me such pleasurable, soul-seeking sensations.

Never before had I ever known an equal to this.

Until now, Roland's organ was only partially inserted. A little at a time I felt more of it struggling to enter! My coozie tried to aid by sucking it in. I began to feel my spend approaching! I did so badly want to prolong that moment. Merciful God! I thought my heart would explode! Oh how my vaginal tube squeezed together—so tight! A wonderful, unexplainable, ecstatic bolt suddenly electrified me. Then something seemed to snap in my vaginal tube and a flood of pasty liquid poured forth. At the same time my cuntie's neck expanded and contracted several times. Each time it did this a new thrill shot through my body. I could plainly feel it nipping the head of Roland's inward travelling monster. I found the sensations overwhelmingly blissful. I wish I could describe it so one could feel it. All I can say, there is no word that can be equal to the joyful cunt-throbbings of a splendid come! It is the one thing that I know which defies description.

This happened just as my cuntie was beginning to get used to the tremendous joint it was sucking in. I really wanted to prolong the climax. Only about three inches of his turgid, throbbing mass was in me when this ecstatic wave made my whole body quiver in delight. Never before had I ever experienced such rapturous emotions. Oh, but, they were glorious!

Even now, as I sit and write my memoirs, and in spite of the hundreds of all kinds of fuckings since, I can plainly hear my frenzied shouts, cries, and moans of my first prick-caused spend!

"Oh—oo—ooo—Oh—oo—ooo—ah ... Roland! Oh dear ... I ... ooo—oo—Oh, how lovely! More! Push it in more ... ah—h—h! Roland, you sure can fuck! Please! Oh fuck me to death! Oh, how wonderful! Mmm—mm—mmm—ah—h—h!" Then everything became blurred and my body trembled convulsively with pleasure. Then my legs gave away and I came down full weight upon his prying peter. Another series of delightful moans escaped my lips.

Then it was Roland's turn to moan: "Keep it up, you beauty. Oh, you wonderful piece of ass! Come give my cock a bath in your girlish virgin juice. Enjoy it again pet, I haven't come yet!"

His eight inches of palpitating stiffness was now into me to its very roots. His hard, hairy balls tickled my bottom and my cunnie lips. I was ravished by sensual delirium. I almost feared that I was dreaming. Could real pleasure be so great?

I heard Roland speak again, in an excited, but mellow voice:

"Oh you, oh darling! You peachy little cunt!'

He began increasing his speed. He pulled his big cock in and out so fast that the friction singed the walls of my prick-lover.

"You, my delicious—your cunt, it's wonderful!" he continued, as his speed still increased! "My hot little mistress. My lovely little sweet fuckable baby girl! I'm—I'm coming! Flossie! Uh—uh—h . . . mmm—mm . . . Flossie, quick! Fuck me off! Hurry! How wonderful!"

I came out of my trance when I heard Roland say: "Fuck me off." That expression somehow rejuvenates my passions and makes me fiercely erotic. My feet were touching the floor. I braced myself on my toes and reared up to meet his gorgeous tool more intimately. I strained every muscle in my legs and back, but in and out his rammer went. I could feel the head of his dick begin to swell. My cunt began to stretch with it.

I answered his erotic outburst:

'I am so glad you think me fuckable, beloved. I am going to do my best to make you feel good too. You made me feel so grand when I came. Oh—ooo—I think I'm going to come again."

"Hold your dress up, girlie. I want to see your cuntie sucking! How delicious it sucks my prick! What a pretty white belly! What nice hairs around your cuntie. Oh how I'd like to suck and kiss your silky hairs!"

I continued moving up and down on his splendid affair. Each time I arose I almost let his tool completely out. I could appreciate the gigantic size of it this way. I could tell how tight I was because I had great difficulty in moving up and down. The friction caused by the barbed disc of his swollen penis was maddeningly thrilling. No woman knows the titilating and exciting feeling of a big, hard, bulbous knobbed penis with little ticklers or "grabbers" on the end of it. No, not until she has one, can it be described!

While working, I noticed that I was the possessor of a rare gift: the art of twisting a man's cock. With every down motion I circled my bottom. This movement set a strange apparatus in my cunnie to work, that nipped and hugged the end of his dick and when I came completely down on his big prick my nippers would hold it so tight it would twist as I spiralled my bottom. Roland howled with delight:

"Oh, baby! HOW YOU CAN FUCK!— I'm . . . I'm coming! Girlie it's the hot joice coming! Oh, God, keep it up! Oh—ah— h—uh!"

My lover grunted as he was spending. He acted like a maniac. He closed his eyes. Each time a spasmodic jet of hot white spew shot into me, he groaned and cried in delight. Did I feel those lava-like loads of juice steaming in and splashing against my uterus walls? I'll say I did. They continued to splash against my walls until I went off again.

In my paroxysms of pleasure my cunnie sucked and pumped every drop of that thrill-containing juice from him. My coozie seemed dreadfully thirsty for that rich creamy effusion that my lover so generously sprayed me with. I screamed from sheer ecstasy. Lord, but it felt good!

Like mad, I began to heave, shove and roll my fat bottom with lightning-like rapidity. My ever lustful cunnie circled and rubbed his cunt-crazy prick until I had many luscious spends. I brought my lover to another point of coming. How he heaved and trembled as he neared his second spewing goal! How he uttered, swore, and moaned during our long, pleasurable frigging orgy. Roland's tool lost none of its power during this time, but continued with its task as big, fat, and turgid as ever. I continually jerked and pumped it; soon I knew I would feel those precious drops of hypnotic spew sending spasms through my whole system. His balls had begun to get hard once more. I took them in my hands playfully and squeezed. I wanted it all! Yes, every drop that my lover's bag contained. His balls got harder and harder! Would they break?

His dick's head swelled and sent forth another creamy supply of love's dearest juice into my drinking cunnie. Gee, my pussy loved that stuff!

He fell on me limply. I felt more—oh double the pleasure, for my performance. I had made a man past the age of youthful vigour spend twice—two wonderful cunt-flooding times! I gloated over his utter abandon and his expressions of lascivious satisfaction. Never since have I seen a face so distorted by lust. His eyes rolled deliriously as he lay prostrate on me after the climax of this long drawn out feast of the flesh. What a ravishing spend he must have had!

I gazed with carnal satiation upon this wealthy, amorous man as he lay helpless and spent upon me. He was completely at my mercy. I still insisted upon tightly holding the remnants of his once prodigious hard-on, now soft but thick, within my steaming slit. The very thought of it in my cunnie and the pleasure that it had afforded me made me come. For the seventh time I gave him my dew! Then I slumped backwards in a semi-swoon, hugging Roland mightily. At the same time I allowed his shrunken tool to slip from my inundated and passion-charred pussy. What heavenly bliss!

We reclined there on the seat too exhausted to move. I was entrapped in his arms. We were both enjoying the afterglow and the soothing dying-away, as we sped on through the countryside.

I emerged from my trance as dear Roland began to wipe my sensitive crack with his soft silken handkerchief. He also offered me a sip of brandy which he said would help me regain my strength.

Believe me, my friends, that was some auto ride!

He too, soon recovered his aplomb. He lavished me with extravagant praises. In a voice faint and tender he spoke:

"Flossie, dear, I am a most fortunate man. I am more than that, for I have possessed a creature so lovely and so tempting. You are absolutely the most skilful and the most perfect little fucker that I have ever humped. Oh, how you can screw! I have had women in every land but you excel them all, not only in your ability to out-fuck them, but also in beauty, shape, and girlish charms. When we dine, Flossie, darling, I will drink to the most perfect woman in the world."

We made many oral plans for the future. As he talked he fondled my legs and bubbies. Suddenly he raised my skirt above my waist. He drew me closer to him so that he could pet and feel my lily-white, soft bottom. As he molded the cheeks with his hands he spoke:

"What a handsome bottom you have, baby girl. I know it is beautiful." He patted and squeezed the tender, pliant halves.

"Now, Roland," I billed sweetly, "how can you know? You haven't had a real good look at it yet."

"Girlie, I don't have to see it. I JUST KNOW! After performing so well, you know the old saying, "What works beautifully must be beautiful.' You've heard of it?"

I kissed him furiously again, and ran my tongue far into his mouth. It was my turn to do the complimenting:

"Now, Roland, darling, I don't wonder why you have women and girls galore. Anyone with a cock like yours could win an entrance to any cunt. It doesn't make any difference whether the pussy is a part of the juicy body of a sixteen year old anxious-to-fuck maiden or the worn and particular cunt of the old maid of fifty.

"Your prick is a darling. It's the kind that I have always dreamed of having ever since I learned the use of the male stiffness. That's been I guess since I was sixteen." I lied, because I knew that the night before last was my first lesson of its real use.

"Not that it makes any difference, but tell me, Flossie, dear, how did you lose your maidenhead? I don't think I took it."

"Honestly, Roland, you are the first man I ever fucked. Do trust me!"

Then I told him how it happened, how a girl friend of mine at school used to rub my twat with hers and one day she got so excited that she jammed her whole hand in between my lips and I felt something break. I grew very scared because blood flowed from the punctured place. I was very cautious never to allow my hand to slip in that region again for fear of rupturing some blood vessel.

All this I told him in my usual innocent girlish way. The tale caused him to become so passionate that his cock grew very stiff and big again. I too became hot. We thought that we were going to have another round of frigging but we neared instead the famous Palais D'Coite, the place where we intended to dine. We postponed the promise to be and rearranged our attire. A mad impulse seemed to sway Roland. He picked up my dress and kissed my belly, clitty, and sucked my lips with all his cunt-satisfying might. Then he combed my curly pussy hairs through his teeth.

Hooligans! All this made me feel hotter than hell! I cannot keep cool when a person kisses me that way, for I do love it so! I almost went off again, but the car pulling into the driveway of our destination prevented any furtherance of Roland's operations.

We straightened our clothes again and stepped from the car. We looked as respectable as anyone else. I guess we were like everybody else. We were aware of the fact that we fucked and we were aware of the fact that we had a pussy and prick. Isn't it foolish how we as well as everyone try to cover those facts with a filmy sheet of garment? After all, it would be different if everybody's pussy and prick were of radically different shapes, and it was embarrassing to another to describe his or her organ. But we know how they look and we know everbody has one, so what in the world is the use of hiding it? Oh, well, I guess it is a funny world.

❧ 3 ❧

3

We entered the Palais D'Coite. It was a most
attractive tavern with hotel atmosphere.
Roland registered, then we were led to a
"private dining room," that is, it was called
that by the host. In reality it was a sumptuous bedroom with a table elaborately set
for dinner. I was awe-struck by the dreamy
effect in the appointment of the room.

At the end of this chamber, furtherest from
the door, was an inviting bed. How I would
like to get laid on it, I thought.

Apparently this room was carefully made
for fuckers only. The ceiling above the bed
was mirrored! The foot and the head of the
bed were similarly fitted.

Heavy damask drapes hung alongside the
bed. They could be drawn and completely
hide the bed. I presumed that this arrange-
ment was made for bashful parties, or else
to help muffle the lustful shrieks and cries of
passion maddened fuckers.

Dim red lamps cast a sensuous, glowing
pallor throughout the room. With such

atmosphere who would not become passionate? I know my cunt was glowing with the same red pallor of the room.

Evidently the dinner was arranged beforehand. It was served as soon as I removed my white wrap and tam.

Roland locked and bolted the doors, then he kissed me with the fervour of youth in its wildest stage. I opened my dress so that he could obtain a more complete view of my, until-a-few-minutes-ago, virgin charms. He dashed his lips to my white, plump bubbies and tried to suck them thin. I was already hot enough to receive his bursting dick, but he spoke:

"First we'll drink a love potion and eat a hearty meal . . . it feels even better than."

"Why, beloved, could anything feel any better than that we have both indulged in? It was so divinely heavenly." I looked at him with a hazy lustful expression in my eyes.

"With such alluring atmosphere and you, the zenith of seductiveness, I, in this room expect to reach the highest height of joys, the crowning fuck of my life." He spoke poetically and in utmost sincerity.

He gripped me in his arms again and caressed me with artistic grace. It touched me as no other kiss ever did. Then we began our meal.

First we drank two delicious cocktails. They reminded me somewhat of my first drink with Don, my former flame. How different everything here was compared to that dingy little speak-easy, and how different a girl I was then. He tried to put his hand on my knee then. I slapped his face and I cried. Now I dared anything, just to cool an itching pussy. Funny isn't it, how a girl's morals change in so short time?

Never before had I looked at a meal that made me seethe between the legs, but this meal did! What a dinner! I later learned that the dishes were chosen to produce this result. Not only did they cause one's passions to rise by gazing upon them, but they were of such constituents that they created abnormal secretions of the love juices and increased the promotion of erotic feelings.

I assume that every man and woman who fucks knows that the more love syrup a man or woman has the hotter they get and the longer they fuck; even the feeling is greater. This meal was more or less an appetizer for the coming feast of the flesh.

When I had finished about half of my meal, and the many flavoured wines, I was drunk, not from the alcoholic contents of them, but from the strange, passion-exciting elements that they contained. I was "raring" to fuck. I would have disrobed in the middle of a public thoroughfare or park if I knew that would get me the big prick that I now so impatiently yearned for.

We both were nibbling on oysters when Roland seized another little bottle of champagne, as though some idea suddenly struck his mind. He reached for the glasses, his eyes at the same time gloated over my bared titties. He filled two of them to the brim and spoke:

"Here is to a fascinating girl, with a ravishingly beautiful form and a bewitching cunt, may she forever be mine, and full of spunk, right now she's hot and full of shot!"

We did not drink. I wanted to get a toast out of my mind with even more lust than Roland's. I was continually getting warmer between my legs, my cunnie was burning, itching, and genuinely cock-hungry. I picked up my glass, as did he, and through my passion-dimmed eyes I dreamily gazed into his and declaimed:

"Here's to my lover,
    A king of a shover;
His supply of cream,
    In my cunt shall stream;
Such floods of delight,
    I want every night;
His cream is like dew,
    It will always make me spew;
May he reign supreme,
    Of his prick I will dream!"

Just fancy a demure girl, with an innocent, baby-face of twenty springing a toast like that. I actually blushed at my unprecedented boldness. You should have seen Roland's face when I finished. It had that, baby-I-could-fuck-you-to-death, expression written all over it. The way he rushed around to my side of the table I thought he was going to eat me. He milked both of my titties, first with his hands then with his mouth. We were both the worse from the bubbie stimulating exercise. Then he released me and panted:

"You lovely cock-stimulator, I'll finish my dinner with your cream puffs!"

He again bent and sucked on the stiff red nipples, sending many more shivers of delight through me. I almost wet my chemise, but Roland stopped just as I felt my tube beginning to contract. I really didn't want to come then because I wanted to save every drop of luscious spend for the dessert to this meal . . . our cunt and prick embrace. Besides, when I come I always want a big throbbing prick between my legs.

I wanted to surprise Roland with the same kind of attack that he visited upon me. Impulsively I dashed to his side of the table and before he was fully aware of my purpose I had unbuttoned his trousers and bared his bursting cock. I tenderly fondled it with my hands, then I found its eye with the tip of my flaming tongue. Roland squirmed and groaned under the spell of this attack. After swabbing the head lightly with my tongue I put the entire crown in my mouth. I drew my lips very firm and held them in that position for a few minutes. Then slowly I drew my lips, keeping them tight all the time, until they freed his stormy peter. Roland almost came.

"Now, Roland, I've repaid you. Now sit down and eat, please! If you show me that big handsome thing of yours again I'll go off in my panties. You know, dear, when I go off I want every bit of you in me."

We continued our dinner as my lover gazed at my fat little titties. Those two springy mounds of flesh with their insidious red nipples standing outward perkingly, were reminiscent of two little hard-as-iron peters.

"Gee-whizz, girlie," Roland said feverishly. "I could feast on your titties forever! How I would like to fuck you between those two appetising mounds of meat! And how wonderful it would be to watch my juice flood your immaculate neck and trickle over to put cream on your two ripe strawberry nipples. Baby, I'm cunt crazy! You are the cause! I can hardly wait . . . oh I'm going to fuck you so good!"

These words streamed right through me; starting at the nipples of my tits, they sent an electric thrill down to my itching slit between my legs.

Just before we finished our dinner, Roland opened another bottle of wine and proposed the following:

"If my little queen will do the belly dance

upon the table, then she will be my choice to take across the sea with me! Here's to Flossie, the queen of belly dancers!''

I wasn't shocked, but I certainly was surprised—who wouldn't be! A trip to Europe just for a belly dance. I never had seen an actual performance of this requested dance, but did I balk? I should say I didn't!

I gave the room a hasty look to determine whether it was possible for anyone other than Roland to witness the exhibition. Even the keyhole had a covering. I trembled as I mounted the table, not for fear of being caught amid this lascivious dance, but I was not confident whether I could perform this feat well enough to merit the promised trip abroad. After all, I had only heard of this dance, yet I formed a mental opinion of its description. That is all I had to go by. I wanted to do my best to please my man.

I removed all my clothing, except my slippers and stockings. I had always thought that shoes and hose add to the seductiveness of the nude feminine form. I opened and closed my legs at the thigh joints, thus teasingly revealing my red-lipped cuntie. You should have seen Roland! How he gloated! His eyes burned with a passionate fire and bulged from their sockets.

I glanced in the mirror to see the effect that I must be causing in Roland. My God! I created a scene that would make any man drunk with lust, let alone one with Roland's cunt-loving nature. It was brazen, but what in the hell did I care. For a trip abroad this was merely a down payment. I would have performed an act ten times as rash if I was asked to do so. Didn't I want to go stark nude in the public park just for a big, fat, juicy prick between my legs?

Roland blew me a kiss, then he applauded. I then kicked off my slippers so that I would be more certain of my footing. I posed for a moment with my legs apart. I knew that my swollen slit composed a tempting picture. I was certain that through the strands of silky protection my vaginal mouth beckoned my lover's lust to higher spheres of uncontrollable desires. Its moist and pulpy lips protruded plainly through those soft, silky, protecting hairs.

I do not think it is necessary for me to describe the dance as everyone has probably seen it. I have described how I looked upon the table. You can imagine how nice my plump bubs looked shaking in every direction. And Roland said that it was worth a million dollars to watch my pussy whirl. He told me that every time I moved down the mouth opened and as I went up it closed.

My audience could bear the scene no longer. He pulled out his beating cock and began to shake it in every direction. It grew very large and glowed with lust again. I was so fascinated by this I almost forgot to continue with my act. He kept his eyes fixed on me. He muttered and panted in glowingly eloquent terms, approval and encouragement. This made me hotter and wilder; as a result my movements were becoming more frenzied and more distorted. I guess if my pussy wasn't grown in me I would have shaken it from its folds.

I raised my hands and placed them behind my head. Then I elevated my juicy shaft so that my cunt-hungry admirer could look deep into my fiery slit. I cried to him:

"Rollie, dear, make yours come, I want to see it shoot!"

I went through the motions of fucking as I had watched him going through the lewd ceremony. If I were really jazzing someone I imagine that I would have been one hot and furious fuck. All this brought me to a point of maddening, erotic feeling. I felt that if I saw him come I too would spend.

Roland's hand began to more tightly clutch his peter. Its knob grew more purple and swollen, to the point of bursting. His hand increased its speed, then he moaned:

"Flossie, are you look—I—I'm—Ah—I'm coming! Here she comes! See it squirt! Oh, how good it feels! Ah—h—uh!"

He went off. It looked like milk pouring from a cow's teats. He shot all over the table, floor and a few drops found my spew-thirsty slit. His balls elevated and sank. Each time they went through this movement a machine-gun-like barrage of sperm came flying out of his one eyed crater, scattering at tangents; more or less a volcanic eruption in miniature.

When the last drops of his creamy dew ran over the part that divides the two sides of his cock's head, I dashed from the table to his side. I placed the turgid spew-sopped knob of his bobbing pole in my mouth. My, oh my! I have never till then tasted anything so delicious as his sperm-oiled reeking knob . . . and remember, I had just finished one of the most appetising meals that I had ever eaten. This was incomparably more ravishing! I guess I am a girl who is far more spew-hungry than food-hungry. How I sucked those last drops of priceless cream! Roland writhed in agonizing ecstasy!

In a trembling voice he moaned:

"Suck it all out, girlie. Oh, God! How lovely it is! How ravishing!"

His strength ebbed as I continued with this operation. He fell into a submissive swoon, and still I continued to extract the remnants of his salty, deliciously warm, precious fluid. I swear by Eros it was good!

This action did not tend to subside my fires. When I had finished, the itch in my cunnie had grown to giant size. My pussy was craving to be prick-crammed.

I poured a cordial for Roland, who now seemed faint and weak. Instead of swallowing the drink he merely sipped the brim so that it would not overflow. Then, as though he had regained all his vim he picked me up, carried me over and placed me on the bed. He assured me that my quim would not be neglected, but it must have a drink.

Roland quickly undressed. I must confess that his body revealed youth and true masculinity—well-formed and apparently strong muscles, suggesting a member of a daily calisthenics class. His skin was baby-white and well covered with hairy patches. It seemed as though nature had awarded my lover more than his share of male qualities. The one feature of his that attracted me most of all was his superbly handsome prick. It was as fat, long, and juicy looking now as it was before his recent spend. It protruded from his large, bewhiskered balls like a drum-major's baton . . . in fact, it beat like one too. Of course, I wondered how long could his remain in that position.

After he had removed all of his clothing he took the glass of cordial in his hand and approached the bed.

"Now open your legs, sweet," he commanded.

I could think of no other request that I would have welcomed more at that time. His orders clicked perfectly with my mood. I raised my plump, little lily bottom, thus elevating my pulsating pussy, and propped my knees high and wide. My cunt section was about six inches in the air. He gazed longingly and carnally at my stretched, spew-thirsty slit, which was so wantonly exposed to his cunt-seeking view. His eyes glared like two spotlights! In puzzled anxiety I awaited his movements. He placed two fingers within the lips and pried them apart. His warm touch made my pussy twitter. My tube opened and closed in anticipation. Oh mercy, how my orifice flamed! Upon my word, it felt like it was really burning! It might have been my imagination, but I sensed steam rushing through my pulsating vaginal tube and bursting past my two swollen, red, pliant lips.

Roland was now observing my smacking lips more closely, he watched them open and close. A maniac's carnal smile beamed from his lips. What the hell are you going to do? I wanted to ask. I was lust-crazed. A fast fuck is what I needed much more than anything else in the world. Give it to me you god-damned cunt teaser!

I'm glad I didn't speak that impulsive thought. Even if I would have, I wouldn't have been at fault. Most girls know how insanely lustful they become when they are played with this way and the prick is meditative about entering. In this condition all women want to be transfixed by the biggest, meatiest and most heated prick in the world—or available at the time. Yes, and they have a desire to swim in the ecstatic pools of nectarious spew.

As my coozie opened once more, Roland

dashed the entire glass of cordial into the depths of my delirious cunt. Then he held the lips together to allow the juice to penetrate into the innermost depths of my womb. At first this cunt drink soothed and cooled, but, God! As soon as it reached my uterus, a million bugs—no a billion—were biting and scratching at the walls of my interior nest!

"Christ, Almighty, God, Roland, I'm going crazy!" I screamed, as I underwent this experience.

Without a doubt this was the wildest frenzy of passion that I have ever undergone. Surely, I thought, I would either die or be left a life long prick-o-maniac! I couldn't even faint to escape this delightful torture.

"Roland!" I exclaimed, "Goddamn! Roland! Do Something! Oh for Christ's sake! I'm going nuts! Oh I'm dying! Please!" Then I cried in delirium, "God have pity on my soul, I know I . . ."

I did not finish my last sentence, because Roland had begun to answer my pleas. He dropped to his knees and with the skill of a master, glued his lips to my open cunnie mouth, and before any of this passionate fluid escaped, he began to suck. He drank every drop from my burning chambers.

He began to ravish my pussy with his lips and tongue. How I craved for a spend! Only God and I know, I cannot explain this to anyone.

His lips, tongue, and tickling moustache were now beginning to be an even greater stimuli than the cordial. I crossed my legs around his head and drew his jabbing dart further into my nest. If I was to obey the dictates of my will at that moment I would have drawn his entire head within my slit and have him wiggle his ears. Ye Gods! How he did suck and lap me! He paused now and then, increasing my frenzied yearnings to come.

His skilful performance of this act had its telling effect upon me. I began to screw my plump little ass around. I let my left leg slip from his neck and fall upon his gigantic bolt. I tickled the bottom of my foot on the head of his red-hot peter; it was truly hot, because it almost burned the sole of my foot. Gosh, but it was hard! Just as rigid as a bone. Its undulating motions rocked my foot up and down. It seemed as though his kissing and tongue-garnishing my cunnie had caused his lust to continually rise. I rubbed my limb all over the crown of his rock.

I soon felt my climax nearing, so I cried in pants:

"Rollie! Oh, Rollie, dear! Ah! Uh, so good! Put your tongue in further! Oh, faster! Faster! Rollie! How nice . . . you suck and tongue-fuck me so nicely! Ah-h-h-ooo-ah-h-uh-h!"

Goddamn, but it was good! Gee-zoo, but I loved it so! Since he knew that my climax was approaching he began to tickle my asshole with his finger and work his dagger with more zeal. I again began to hug him with my legs, firmer and firmer as the spend neared. Boy, it was getting good!

The floodgates of love at last released my dew! I panted, writhed, and murmured, as I convulsively opened and closed my thighs about his neck. I strained the muscles of my belly, each time my spasmodically contracting cunnie sent out a delicious dose of love's sweet syrup. The feeling of gratification overtook me, but only momentarily . . . only too soon I wanted his dick in my cunt.

After he had completely lapped my discharge, he sealed his task with a soul-satisfying upward sweep with his tongue. He arose from his kneeling posture, his dick still lust-swollen. Any other girl would have expired from fright at the sight of this gigantic prick, but not I. This scene kindled another blast of ecstasy in my reeking twat. Gosh, I thought, and this is only the beginning! I had just begun to enjoy the qualities of a genuine lover. I gloated over him as I spoke:

"Oh, Roland dear, what a beauty it is! I can't understand how such a big thing gets into so small a place. How are you going to get it into me?"

"I'll show you, you sweet fuckable baby. You're beginning to make me wish that I was only twenty again. Raise your fat little ass! That's the nice little girl."

He placed a pillow beneath, thus setting my fucking machinery in a more convenient position. He also placed another one under my head so that I could view the procedure more easily. Now we were all set for a comfortable and lingering jazz. Was I holding my breath? I'll say I was, and I was also holding my cunnie mouth open in readiness to gobble up the approaching explorer. I could plainly feel my nervous lips quiver in anticipation.

Roland caught both of my legs and strung them through his arms. He picked my plump, baby-skin thighs up so that the part was on the same plane with his bursting cock. I watched the operation from the mirror in the ceiling. My pussy was growing more and more impatient. When he had found the level that was most advantageous he refixed the padding that propped my bottom. Taking his monster dick in one hand he put it close to my kitten's mouth; with the other hand he parted my crop of blonde silky, interwoven hairs.

He placed his swollen purple-knobbed prick within the meshy folds of my pliant cunt-lips. My blood tingled with delight! For a moment he playfully fondled his dick-head in my juicy slit. He also rubbed it zealously against my clitty. I was excited to the point of insanity by the hypnotic influence of his pulsating giant.

After getting it well lubricated in the sap of my vent he sank it in the orifice of my pouting vagina. I could not prevent myself from lunging for this ramming rool with my hand, such was my excitement. At last it found its goal. My cunt yielded submissively to this terrific thing . . . such ravenous zest! He assisted my hand; in fact, he prevented my hand from making his instrument drive inward with fierce, cunt-ripping force. With the skill of a master he slowly, gently and almost painlessly drove his big Bertha home.

As it tunneled its way in and in—God, the pleasure was great!

I now realise how much I could have spoiled my pleasure had I been allowed to do my will, that is, rush his in with brutal force.

Only the women who have been fucked by master screwers are able to understand the soul-stirring thrills and sensations of a big, oh, such a nice, sweet dick that is buried slowly and sensually into the depths of a super-sensitivie pussy well.

Roland trembled as he spoke:

"How delightful! What a wonderfully tight pussy you have! Gee, baby, am I hurting you, Flossie?'

"Yes, but I love it! It feels so good. Oh, how I love your big fat thrilling prick—it's so damn good!"

When he had sunk his full eight inches into me, Roland allowed it to rest in that position for a few moments. I could feel the pulse in his prick, making it swell and bob. This provided a most absorbing and delightful thrill. Slowly his big cunt-cork began to pull out. It fitted so snugly in my tube that it felt like it was dragging—no—causing to collapse, the structure that holds my internal organs intact.

Whenever I think of that feeling I am always blessed with a coating of hot dew in my slit. You, dear reader, can rest assured that as I pen these words I have at my service many big-pricked men fully capable of satisfying the many cunt-heating attacks that I have so far experienced and will continue to, during the course of writing this book.

As I have said he was slowly drawing his cock from my slit. When he had drawn it almost completely out he shoved it in again with a most terrific lunge. He repeated his action; each time he accelerated his speed. Back and forth it glided; at every stroke his magnificent mass of glorious stiffness caused me to make short outcries of "ohs," and "ahs," etc. A wave of ecstasy, which was produced by that hard raspiness under the knob, began at my coozie and ripped up my belly to my chest. There it would fade in the heavings of my bosom and the beating of my heart.

It was all so heavenly, I wished to prolong the agony of delight . . . oh, so badly.

He changed his course again. He drew it almost completely out, let it rest in that position for a short time, then he would take it and rub it between my quivering lips. Sometimes he would press it to my swollen clitty. With renewed lust, he would, with terrific force, dash it into the depths of my slit-tube.

Spend? I spent almost every time he plugged my hole in this manner.

The curtains were of little use. They certainly couldn't muffle my loud shrieks of unprecedented ecstasy.

The friction that is so overwhelming to the average woman was more than that to me. I could neither control nor prolong any of my comings. Every time I shot I became so overcome by the extreme pleasure that I lost my senses in momentary deliriums; that can be partly blamed, if not entirely on the spasmodic contractions of my vaginal tube. Gee! My whole belly seemed to squeeze whenever this happened.

I wondered how he could hold back so long. Imagine, all this time he retained his load! He withheld his pleasure for a time that seemed like a half hour—it might have been longer. One never knows how much time passes when one is engaged in frantically emotional jazz.

His face glowed with a handsome pallor as he watched his tool appear and disappear into the depths of my come-soaked slit. He gloated over the spicy picture of us in the nearby mirror.

It was maddening. After being engaged in such lechery and lust for so long a time, in spite of this fact, he still withheld that precious fluid. I was actually hungering for another load of his hot juice to revarnish my womb. Would he ever come?

He suddenly picked me up while his largeness was still in me and swung my legs over his shoulders. This spread my knees even farther apart. My fat, rubbery thighs held his neck snugly between them. How we ever managed to get tangled in that position, even Roland didn't quite understand. At any rate it gave his prick more freedom to work. It felt now, like even his balls were caught in my prick-trap.

Up, up, up, I puckered my crazed cunt . . . even his balls weren't enough to satisfy me. I wanted his whole body in my little twat. God, what made me so prick crazy? I didn't know. I guess it was what is commonly called "fuckinebriation." I pushed my legs and stretched them, anything to make the gap between my knees greater— ever pushing my cunt up to meet my big visitor more intimately.

I thought that I had enjoyed jazzing in the old way but it was nil compared to this new position.

He paused long enough during these thrusts to kiss me with all the fervour of his cunt-inflamed soul. He also moulded my bubbies with his hands.

"Flossie, what exquisite titties!" he exclaimed, then kissed me between my plump mounds "and how deliciously you can fuck. Flossie, you are gorgeous. Oh-oh. Bite me with your cunt-teeth! Eat it! Girlie, it's so good! Oh, you hot cunt! I'll . . . I'll . . . fuck you full of love juice . . ." and he continued muttering between these entrancing deep digs and twists.

I was speechless and could only gasp with convulsive thrills.

"Oh . . . ah . . . Take that! And that! Oh boy! mmm-mm!"

He sprayed his strong jets of creamy fluid into me. God, it made me tremble so! He slowed down, closed his eyes and sank upon me. He wallowed in my arms and legs, panting in profound ravishment. This, a man enjoys so very much especially after he has shot a woman full of his nectar-like fluid.

Roland did not have a better spend than I, nor did he enjoy the feast as much as I. How could he? I experienced ten of the most heavenly and satisfying spends that I have ever had.

I lay there cuddling him in my nude arms

and body, with his big, fat, bobbing cock still buried in me.

We were thus both enjoying the aftermath of this delicious fucking.

For over an hour we played with each other's fineries. Roland sucked my firm nipples until I was tempted to ride again with his big, fat jock stuffed snugly between my plump thighs.

To excite my lover to another erection I toyed and fingered his enormous bag, digging my fingers into the sensitive nerve roots. I stimulated his imagination with vivid, enticing lewd word-pictures of the fucking affairs that lay before us. I also described to him how irresistibly desirable I would always keep myself in the future.

It was then that I had begun to study him more carefully. I wanted to understand him perfectly; his every sexual desire as well as the exact extent and strength of his libidinous nature. I guess I did this for some very good but indistinct reason. Maybe it was because I once heard my aunt say that the best and only way to hold a man was by his prick, or something to that effect. At any rate I was determined to discover for myself how and when he wanted his cunt. With all my mind, with all my soul, with all my heart, and with all my cunt I was desirous of holding my cherry-smasher. Wasn't he the one experienced prick in a million?

I sought every artifice by which I could hold his fancy and arouse his lustful emotions.

I concentrated my efforts then on making his indulgence in my arms as highly seasoned with sensational spiciness as my immature knowledge would permit. I put his still soft knob in my pussy. Soon life flowed into it. The once soft head, which was now sheathed deeply into my vent was again beginning to throb and bob. It wasn't long until it stiffened to its original bigness.

To feel a man's cock expand within you and grow stiff is a most unusual sensation. Its slow, but steady widening in my vaginal walls made me burn with a fever to fuck. Lord, but I was aching to jazz some more! I had become so randy that I bit his face and chewed his tongue.

Roland did not mount me as he did previously. Instead we remained lying on our sides in such a position that he could conveniently play with my baby-skinned thighs and fat round bottom. He watched my pussy as it swallowed his enormous, fat dick. The screwing which immediately followed was an unforgettably voluptuous one. He kissed my lips and sucked my titties as he pumped his steaming hot jock into my welcoming womb.

This was another occasion when I spent many times before he painted my uterine walls with his hot jets. How wonderful it was to once more feel the full force of his juice-sprayer. Unrelentlessly it pumped his hot balsamic load into me. He wallowed in my cunnie after each spasmodic jet of hot sperm was ejected and cried:

"You delicious cunt! I could fuck you forever . . . God, but it feels good!"

My nippers operated perfectly on his shooting prick. Soon they had extracted all the juice of this come.

My pulsating quim could no longer retain its glorious fluid, and I, too, spent with much fury. Our emissions thus mixed as I extracted his last drops with my pussy's pliers.

We sank into a delicious oblivion, then we prepared ourselves for our return trip.

During the entire journey home, he coddled me in his arms and breathed many sweet expressions into my ears. He also spoke of the promised trip abroad, of London and Paris. With such beautiful words he embroidered these places that it appeared to me that we were, in reality, to embark on a voyage to an earthly paradise.

We reached home about ten-thirty that evening, sealing one of the most heavenly episodes of my life.

Aunt Stella was anxiously awaiting my return. I introduced Roland to her. I assumed that her eagerness for me to arrive home was not one that was founded on worry for my safety, but a strong curiosity to know how my experience turned out and to learn the answers to the usual barrage of questions, such as: "How did you like it? Did it feel good? How did his thing look? Was it nice and big? How long did you go? How many times did you come?" and etc.

I perceived Roland gloating over the voluptuous charms of my aunt.

Men are funny creatures, aren't they? No sooner do they exhaust themselves fucking one woman, than as early as five minutes later they want to screw another dress-covered, well-set, ass-and-bubbied torso.

To themselves they say: "Gosh, but I'd like to try that. I'll bet she'd make some hot jazz!"

Some women are that same way about men. They too want to screw every handsome man that appears to have a big thing in his pants in spite of almost being fucked to a heavenly death a few moments before. I, for one, belong to that group.

Roland didn't suspect it, but on my way home, for every man I saw, I wondered how big his concealed meat-stick might be.

"Was it as big as the cop's club," I would ask myself, referring to the one that hangs about the corner of 42nd St. and Broadway.

Really I couldn't very well blame Roland for shining that want-to-jazz-you light in his eyes. The way Aunt Stella was clad was sufficient to warrant this desire. She wore a transparent kimono which daringly revealed every feature, including her attractive mossy patch. Only this prevented Roland from seeing the happy lips of her cunnie.

If I were to depart from the scene they would have, no doubt, indulged in each other's charms. Anyhow they both looked as though they could enjoy fucking each other, then and there. I was alert to this possible situation . . . I was selfish; I wanted every drop of Roland's sperm, therefore I rushed my seducer from the house under the pretense that the hour was late and that we were both in need of a refreshing sleep. He was not at all pleased because he entertained his desire for auntie's coozie, but he moved towards the door hesitantly.

I was truly ashamed of myself for not letting him spend in Stell's cunt but, as I have written, I wanted every thrill that my lover was able to give me.

After kissing Roland good-night in Stell's presence—and incidentally, this embrace even made my aunt hot—I began to relate to her my adventures in the realms of unchasteness . . . and were they unchaste!

By the time I had reached the end of my tale we were both so cunt-steaming that we were compelled to finger-screw each other twice before we were able to doze into a "dreaming-of-prick-all-night" sleep.

4

4

When Roland asked me to become his mistress I did not hesitate in the acceptance of his offer. Yes, many were the reasons for my affirmative verdict. The most obvious of them all was the fact that I was an orphan with a very meagre income.

Marriage between us was out of the question. He did what he thought was the next best thing: adopted me as his daughter. In that manner we would travel. This action also made me financially secure and gave him the freedom he desired. I guess in this way Roland was more clever than "Daddy" Browning.

My sweetheart's next move was to open an account in my name. He placed ten thousand dollars in it . . . merely a mild beginning. I was instructed to buy with this sum enough feminine fineries to suffice until we reached the shopping centre of the world, Paris.

Literally, I was another Cinderella . . . but my dream continued much longer.

When we reached Paris he settled another similar sum upon my head. Once we had arrived in that city he immediately led me to his sumptuous apartment which was located in the Rue de L'Opera. There I lived in the same luxurious comforts as the world's most touted mistress.

Before continuing further with my adventures in Europe I think I will relate some of the incidents that occurred during my passage across. You, dear reader, will find them of sufficient interest to merit the space I will give them. I did profit immensely from the erudition that I gained during this trip.

During most of the time aboard Roland confined himself to his stateroom. I think he was mapping his plans for the future. Nevertheless, this gave me a great deal of time to myself to roam about unobserved.

My purser was a handsome lad of English origin . . . and very true to his race, I determined later. He was about twenty-four. To me it seemed he had taken an unusual interest in me. His added attention and undue courtesies to me caused me to be thus opinionated.

Whenever I sought my deck chair he would be there at my side ready to tuck the robe about my legs and hips. This task he always performed with deliberate slowness, minutely feeling every inch of my shapely calf as he pinned the robe beneath my body.

At first it seemed to me that this was a part of his routine . . . after all, what did I know about the duties of a purser.

After he had performed his chores a few times he began to show a more intimate attitude towards me . . . not by what he said but by what he did. He nipped my calves as he worked his hands around them. Was this a demonstration of courtesy or desire? If one is fool enough to think it is the former then let one think so. I certainly didn't, even though it might have been done by accident.

This slight stimuli excited my want-to-be-fucked-by-new-pricks emotion. I not only showed my delight in his toying with my legs in this manner, but I also encouraged him with the look in those large flirtatious blue eyes of mine. It was one of those glances which, if interpreted properly, would say:

"Big boy, if you only knew how badly I really wanted to screw you."

At that particular time he progressed no further; I guess he was playing a cautious game. The next time he gave both of my legs a pussy-singeing squeeze and then held them for a long time. At first he shyly avoided looking into my face—perhaps for fear of viewing an expression of contempt or shock. Then, seeing that I did not protest, the next time he looked for my facial reactions to his advances. I felt highly elated: perhaps I showed it, because he thought me friggable. He grew bolder. Who wouldn't if they desired some savoury piece of tail and the owner of that juicy slit didn't object to one's slow approach.

At last he had reached the stage where he would let his hands rove slightly above my knees. He ran them soothingly over my pliant thighs, pressing his thumbs in deeply. The tact with which he did this made this exercise a most cunt-invigorating one.

During all these leg-feels he never uttered a word. This would puzzle the most experienced woman! I began to wonder whether just playing with my legs was satisfying to him or whether he longed for something better.

I wanted a showdown ... what was he aiming at? The best way to determine this was to await his next exploration trip to my thighs and call for an explanation.

The third day out Roland had completely neglected my cunt ... in fact he seemed too fatigued, due more or less to his excessive erotic exercises and business perplexities. You can hardly realize how sorely I was in need of that big, fat, juicy, meat stick between my legs.

Since the purser, whose name I found out was George, noticed that I offered no resistance to his advances, his cunt-seeking hand had become a degree bolder with each performance of his duty.

The day when I was hottest between the

legs, he approached to assist me into my chair.

"Good morning, George," I smiled.

Those were the first words that were spoken between us. He looked at me in surprise, wondering how I learned his name.

"Good morning," he echoed, "jolly pleasant trip we're having."

I had an excellent reason for choosing the isolated spot on deck where I now sat ... today it was going to be either fuck or I'll feed you to the sharks.

I reclined in the long, comfortable chair and awaited for him to cover my bottom and legs with the deck rug. I tried to look as lewd as I knew how. I wore that familiar wanton, submissive grin on my face.

The wind had blown my dress a bit above my dimpled knees, revealing the tempting full roundness of my thighs. This did the trick! Like it was struck by a flash of lightning, his prick bulged in his pants. His eyes portrayed repressed emotions; his extremely nervous hands bespoke his inward desires most profoundly.

George placed the rug at my feet and drew it upward very slowly. When he had reached my dimpled knees he paused, then placed his hands between them. He did this so artfully that if I hadn't seen his prick harden in his pants I would have sworn it was an accident. With his hands still between my knees he continued to draw the rug upward, thus deliberately uncovering my legs as he went. I hoped he wouldn't stop because that day I wore no panties. As his hands crept upward they covered the denuded parts with the rug. When he had reached a distance halfway between my knees and cunt he gave my thighs a sensual nip. It sent a stream of hot fluid gushing out of my crack. My little white thighs quivered under his lustful spell.

I remonstrated, because my intuitive mind fostered the axiom: "Something too easily had is not worthwhile."

"George," I snapped, "you are getting too far above your business. I ought to report you for taking such liberties."

I really felt like saying: you big dope, can't you see I want you to put your big thing between my legs? I want every inch of your big dick shoved all the way in as far as it will go.

"Well," he drawled with typical English nonchalance, "you shouldn't have such a beautiful leg . . . they are too alluring to resist . . . I'm only human, you know."

'So am I, George. You excite me so when you do those things. Honestly, you make me feel like doing something naughty. I should object to your being so familiar. You know you might do something that we'd both be sorry for."

"Miss Flossie, you are naughtily tempting . . . jolly well seductive. Hang it all, let's do that something that you teasingly refer to . . . yes?"

We were, as I said before, well obscured from the crowd. I had found an unnoticed nook on the upper deck.

He sat upon the arm of my chair, an indication that he was serious. In a boyish way he began to court me, first allowing his arm to encompass my neck. Suddenly he tilted my head backwards and planted a seething kiss on my ruby-red lips. I squirmed and gasped, for his lips were genuine charmers to my cunt-sensitive nature.

"George, dear," I gasped, "if you do that again you'll start something—you might be very sorry you kissed me."

As it was not unusual, I was beginning to get hot as hell between my legs. This always happens when I sit near an attractive man, more so when I am kissed by one. I could already feel my cunnie's mouth smacking its lips for this new prick.

The rug had slipped from me, disclosing my tempting legs almost to the border of my hairy slit. My glowing flesh gleamed through the black transparent stockings most appetizingly. Gazing at·them, from the ankle to the naked part of my plump and pliant thighs, George burst forth with none of his usual aplomb:

"Egad, what pretty legs! Can I feel them? By jove, how tempting!"

"George," I snapped as I puckered my

lips pertly, "you men are all so unreasonably careless and hasty. Tell me, just why do you want to feel my legs?"

I then swung my head about girlishly as I casted my eyes at him. I puckered my rosebud mouth to tempt him further.

I must confess that at this point my prick-starved cunnie was beginning to feel those strong itching pains that almost loudly screech my need for a robust cream-emitting cock.

My English friend answered my question by gluing his lips to mine in another fervid, cunt-teasing, prick-raising kiss. Oh, boy! How I wanted to get jazzed, then and there! He trembled with lustful desires in the wake of seething emotions. His hand dove between my locked thighs and worked its way into my silk-curtained box. My bottom involuntarily began to vibrate. I honestly tried to control my feelings and actions as much as it was then possible. This I did because I wanted to be laid in comfort.

I was given to understand that a hustle-bustle jazz wasn't worth the spew or energy that was wasted on it. I knew that if I allowed this already trying situation to grow worse, it would result in a rapid one-shove-and-come jazz. As hot as I was this would have never appeased my mellow-lipped pussy. In spite of this reasoning I could not prevent myself from opening and closing my thighs.

His excitement had overcome every atom of his reserve; in fact, his entire body trembled with heat.

"By jove, dear lady," he uttered in a voice shaking with passionate tremors as he touched my slit, "this is the reason why a man wants to see more of such lovely legs."

I did not reply, but glanced at the object that my heart desired, which was bulging in his tight-fitting trousers. He had a most splendid hard-on. Very plainly, I could see his tool bobbing and jumping as it lay concealed along the side of his leg; my poor pussy, it longed and burned for this apparently savoury tool.

George's finger advanced within my slit. There it wiggled and explored, raising me to the zenith of frenzy. He was panting from his efforts.

"George," I whispered, "you are dreadfully mean. You mustn't do this, you are awfully cruel to tantalize me this way."

To this he replied by taking my hand and leading it to his trousers where he placed it upon his own prick. Feeling it as I did, I discovered that his dick was as hot as fire and as hard as iron.

I was now far too excited to resist any of his advances . . . his finger played freely in my moist cunt-lips while my hand seemed to be magnetized to his hard schmuck. Slowly and unknowingly I was opening my thighs wider and wider. His finger, after it had found its way into my slit, began to glide in and out.

So damned hot was I, from the spell of his fervid touches, that before I could summon sufficient strength to resist, I began to roll my bottom around in the usual fucking-motion fashion. Off I went with a gasp, spending lasciviously over my legs, ass and his hand. During my spasm of pleasure I gave his tool a hard yank, and tight squeeze.

"Oh, my Lord, George," I spurted, as I for the first time realized the true dimensions of his cunt-jabber, "what a ferocious big thing you have . . . what can I do with it?"

"Put it where it belongs! Here . . . in here!" he said as he gave my cuntie a stretch with his still immersed fingers.

"George," I sighed dreamingly, "I wish you could. I hoped you wouldn't think me naughty or bold if I asked you . . . oh I do want you to do it to me so badly . . . you have me so excited, I don't know what to do!"

While I spoke I toyed with his wonderful nuts and tremendous jock.

"Miss Flossie, can't you understand that I'm suffering . . . do something to relieve me. Will you come to my cabin? I know you are afraid to do it out here."

He exposed his tool to my eyes and then kissed me frantically. Thinking that I did not know how to manipulate it, he placed my hand inside his and moved it back and forth over his monster-cock. This action drew the foreskin over his prick-head, then below it. My face was so close to his bounder that I could feel the intense heat radiating from it against my cheek.

Soon he began to moan:

"Flossie, it's so nice! Do it! Do it until I come! You know!"

George again found my hairy gash with two fingers. These he shoved inward as far as they would go. I was frantically passionate . . . in fact, to such an extent that I was brutalizing his peter; I almost jerked it from its socket.

I found it very hard to repress my desire to ask George to fuck me upon the deck, but somehow I managed to find that strength. I had to resign to the tickling of his fingers for that moment. After all, fucking in such a place is extremely dangerous; one can be caught so easily. Aside from this danger I didn't want George to think that I was an easily had jazz.

(Isn't it strange though, when we are hot and even though we know we are going to get well fucked later, we have to screw at the exact place and instance, when and where we are made desirous. Something within us just won't let us take no for an answer. I suppose it's like a lot of things pertaining to the unexplainable matters and problems that we jazzers meet with.)

I was anxious to make George come. I

wanted to see whether he would react to this event in the same manner Roland did. I wished to see, also, whether or not he could shoot farther and more plentifully than my beloved seducer.

(I'm just that way . . . a damned prick-curious, selfish woman. I wanted to examine every handsome man's meat stick and perhaps . . . no, not perhaps, but most certainly, feel them throbbing between my legs.)

It wasn't long until I had George twisting and squirming at the coming point.

"Faster! Faster! Squeeze it! Oh, Flossie, tear it off! Oh how . . . oo . . . ah . . . good!" He panted as his turgid tool began to send forth its hot streams of creamy spew.

I continued jerking until his jock became limp . . . and it did hang limp as a wilted rose after I finished brutalizing his once ravaging monster. After I had completely executed my task he made me promise to visit him in his cabin that night. Everything, he promised, would be arranged so that no one would see me entering his cabin. I knew I couldn't afford to be caught and even pursers might not be permitted to fuck the passengers. What a foolish rule!

After I had fully recovered my senses I began to soberly realize the risk that I had taken . . . if I were to continue this way, the perilous path that I must inevitably follow was also taken into consideration. Was it fair to Roland, to whom I virtually belonged? I certainly could not afford to lose my sole support. Naturally I must decide these problems for always. I rendered a decision: I would keep my present appointment, but in the future, as nearly as it might be possible, I would refrain from such practices.

That evening I made a most careful toilet. As it was my custom, I gave my cunnie a most painstaking douche of mixed incenses. I avoided wearing such surplus clothing as corsets, panties, etc., that the going-to-be-jazzed can get along better without. As a coverall, I wore a simply designed green silk frock—you know, the kind that drapes the form so alluringly. As a safety measure I wore a slip—in event that by some unseen chance I might have been forced to remove my cloak in the light. So you see I did not throw every caution to the wind, just because I was cock-crazy and was on my way to realize a much desired jazz. The stockings I wore were of the black, transparent silk variety. I adorned my feet with slippers, the same shade as my dress.

After examining myself for the last time in my mirror I thought that I composed a portrait that any man would name the "ideal fuck". It did seem to me that my blonde curls embroidering my face made me look more like a doll than a love-to-be-fucked woman.

I thought that I was good enough to delight George to the highest realms. I also hoped that he would not only display a strong desire for my quivering-lipped pussy, but also for my person in general—or was I to be in error? It feels so much better when a man shows his mental desire—plus physical love.

I was most fortunate that evening because Roland had absented himself early under the pretence that he had met an old business crony of his and that he had a supper engagement with him. He explained that it would be boring for me to accompany him, because they were probably going to talk about business, the shipping industry, and so forth.

Intuitively I felt that he had an engagement with another woman, in fact I felt that he was screwing another woman regularly on the boat, not only because of the manner he used in speaking his excuse, but also because of his sudden loss of vitality. Was it his neglect of my quim in favour of another?

After eating supper—really, I drank more than I ate, mostly cordials, which I had learned to love because of their passion stimulating ingredients, since my first drinking them at the Palais D'Coite.

All day long—and it seemed too damn long for I was constantly thinking of that one desirable thing in George's trousers—I was becoming increasingly impatient, in fact by the dinner time I was sorely aching for George to grease his pole in my love balm.

With this added—call it fuel on a hot fire (the cordials), I had no trouble sensing a majestic burning, itching and throbbing in my cunt. If there was ever a time that I needed to get filled, it was at this time. God, but I certainly needed a piece of hot, juicy meat between my legs!

I slipped on a dark cloak, thus making myself as imperceptible as it was then poss-ible in the splendour of that moonlight evening, and I made my way to George's cabin. I knocked:

"Come in, a bea. . . ." He cut short as I appeared.

Obviously, I interpreted his ending his sentence so abruptly as being caused by emotional excitement. Wasn't I the one thing to get excited over? I threw off my cloak, thinking that this (in my analysis) would add to George's excited state.

Apparently the purser did not conceive me the way I thought he did. He spoke again, in a chilled, slightly surprised tone:

"Why, Flossie . . . I . . . I thought you were a full grown woman! Here I discover that you are but a young girl . . . by jove it's embarrassing!"

His mannerisms did not seem like those of the George who wanted me so eagerly earlier in the day. He appeared bashful! Can you imagine that? Did he ever have his prick in a woman's cunt before? I wondered.

Like a novice in nuptial arts he took me in his arms (there was an invisible something in his ways that seemed to say. "Should I do this? No, it's not right, she is too young . . . too much a child.")

He kissed me. It was not a "natural" kiss; it seemed as though he had compelled himself to do this out of courtesy, I guess. It was a stereotyped embrace, lacking all the burning enthusiasm of those earlier in the day.

I was as furious as a tiger . . . passion caused my fury. Like an animal I dug at his lips with mine and lunged upon him. I poured my entire jazz-desiring soul into that one wild, sensuous embrace. I think I would have accomplished more if I had dispelled that intoxicating energy upon an immovable and feelingless stony wall. It didn't budge him from his stoicism. Seemingly enough, his heart was frozen in his chest, his blood iced in his veins, and his spew remained in his balls.

I clung to him almost in despair, yet hopefully. I was famished for a jazz so wild that only my prick-warped imagination could picture it.

I suppose everyone has met with the experience of wanting to screw with all their soul and fucking muscles but not able at the time to quench that libidinous impulse. I know men who have told me that they would like to tear into shreds every stitch of clothing from the bodies of those who cause such uncontrollable wants to rise; similarly, I was seized with an impulse to disrobe my cunt-heater.

During this distorted embrace I slid my tongue between his teeth and it lashed furiously in his mouth. Success was mine, I thought, for as I did this his arms tightened about me and trembled. Encouraged by this, I thrust my tongue to the utmost depths that it would reach in his mouth. By this time, you should have seen my bottom squirm restlessly about, geez whiz! how it itched and burned! My slit was well daubed with the fluids of my sweltering crack, in fact, the juices were streaming down my plump thighs. Now you can understand how imperatively urgent it was that I must have his thing shoved into me. I don't think that I could have been more cock-in-the-cunt-maddened if I had swallowed a large dose of Spanish fly. It was another one of those times when I didn't give a hoot whether I was in the Madison Square Garden before a typical Max Baer audience in the ring with George, I would have jazzed—that's how blindly maddened and I had begun to be. So long as I live I shall never forget that moment.

George didn't even notice my hard bubbies which were now hanging over the top of my dress so alluringly—dynamically desirable to lustful eyes. Had he suddenly turned pansy?

"George," I sobbed hystericaly, "don't you love me tonight? Don't you want me tonight? Please do it . . . do it to me! Aren't you going to do everything you vowed to do on deck today? For God's sake . . . please!"

"Dear Flossie, I'd love to . . . you are so young . . . too young . . . you can't realize what you are about to do.'

"I am young, I know. I look young, but you have aroused a woman's feelings . . . you have made me love you, desire you."

Impressed by my argument, he escorted me to a convenient divan where he sat me upon his lap. He began to feel my titties, knees and thighs. My fat little bottom was also an object on which he expressed his moods. He squeezed and toyed with it, running his hand through my love-to-feel-it crack.

Discovering that I wore no drawers, George became more intimate and aggressive. Soon his trembling and impatient-to-feel-the-twat hand was becoming more intricately involved with my cunnie's kissers. I felt his tool begin to get stiff in preparation for an intimate love duel. In the position in which I then sat his jock was located directly beneath my cream-drinker.

Two of his fingers had already found their way into my crack. His continued explorations didn't quiet my raging fires any—they certainly did stimulate them.

Gee, it certainly was invigorating to feel his rigid tool bounce against my bottom and my silken nest.

"It won't be long now," I consoled myself in silence.

The very flimsy garments that separated my cunnie from his jabber were of little or no protection. I could feel the heat of his inflated knot emitting and trickling readily through my dress to singe the hairs in my crotch. I could stand these pussy titillations no longer and so I gave vent to my feelings:

"Oh, George," I mumbled, half afraid that he was going to refuse my request, "I'll take my dress off . . . yes?"

"Yes, Miss Flossie, we will both undress. I will do it to you even though you are a virgin, but I really shouldn't."

Gosh, either he was just plain dumb, or else I was a maniac with the airs of a virgin, but at a time like this I didn't care to become meditative enough to give this matter a second thought.

It did not take long for us to peel our clothes from our seething bodies, particularly me; I drew my dress and slip off simultaneously.

We both lost no time but hopped into bed as soon as our bodies were denuded. He jumped upon me like a wildcat . . . no preliminaries whatsoever, more like a young animal. Was that the way he took the cherries? Crude indeed, if so.

Some men are hasty; women do not care for them, not those women who can see the beauty in intercourse. Our sex likes the dalliance and the tenderly sweet introductions to the feast of the flesh.

George was primitive and very beast-like. Had I not despaired for that screw so miserably I would have left the scene immediately. I was hurt, yes, and insulted . . . only my hole held his attention. A fuck was my first consideration that night, or might I be permitted to say, a male prick . . . technique ran a distant second.

My English friend was eager to drive his steed home. This he did without any loss of time . . . nor did he care to spare my feelings. No regard for the art. What a pig he turned out to be. He paid no heed to the usual clitty-dick embrace before entering, nor did he allow his jock to converse within my wide-open cunnie's mouth.

It might be reasonable to think that George was a firm convert to the geometric axiom: a straight line is the shortest distance between two points,' that goddamn fool. He must have been if he believed in that befossiled idea and applied it to jazzing!

The more a person fondles with my quim before he sticks his meat in, the more apt he is to find a hotter and more welcoming pussy upon his entering; also, the closer he approaches my heart via this roundabout route. Gee, how detrimental a high school education was to this taking-everything-literally Englishman. At least we Americans do not take our learning that seriously ... or literally.

In order that I might be able to receive a more varied movement from his cock, instead of the stereotyped straight jabbing, I gripped his thing and slid it about in my slit-mouth, then replaced it in my slit proper. When I did this his anxiety was so great to get it back into my tube that he blindly pecked at every wall in the vale between my lips—very brutally. At length, I, like the mother who leads her brood to feed on her tits, if that be the case, had to say as I guided:

"There ... there, in this place ... ow, quick ... oo—you hurt me!"

Never before nor after have I complained of the pains caused me by a ruthless jazzer, not even at the coronation of my cherry removal.

Again, after he had found the proper entrance, he gave his joint a tremendous shove—which, incidentally, was most painful—thus sending his bounding tool home to the roots.

I spent, yes, but it could have been a more enjoyable one. My lover did not seem to, or want to understand that a woman is more than a motionful piece of machinery. Perhaps he thought that because I writhed and screamed that I was enjoying myself to the utmost. The reason I did this was more from pain than anything else.

My pleasure was beginning to mount a second time to another climax, an ending that promised to be far more delightful than any previous one. I assume that it was because I was beginning to get accustomed to his ungraceful tactics.

My judgment this time did not disappoint me ... I was really going to have a most satisfying emission. I knew this positively for I was beginning to feel those indescribably intense throbbings, a feeling that occurs just previous to an ecstatic dew precipitation and soul engrossing spasm. George began to move his tool with more rapid and vicious thrusts, howling with pleasure as he went along. Suddenly he grunted:

"By jove, dearie, I am going to spend!"

The way that damned guy said it burned me up—like he was playing bridge and had made his contract; practical and businesslike.

Yes, I'll admit, the cream did feel delicious but the supply was rather scanty. Roland could have outscored him. Nevertheless this spew bath brought me closer to another spend, a spend that I had been aching to have all day. Another proof that I was going to enjoy this one far better than the first was supplied by another sign, the tugging in my stomach. This sensation I feel, without an exception, previous to a gigantic attack of simmering cunt-wash.

My coozie, during an occasion of this kind, squeezes together with terrific force . . . in fact, so close does it come together that the smallest prick is held immovable in its deathly vice. At the time of coming my stomach feels submerged in undulating spasms as well as bathing in a solution of that magnetic warm, pasty come—just impossibly good.

I was destined to be neglected with this unusual come approaching. Shortly after George's first orgasm his tool began to lose its vigour. It softened, shrunk and wilted until it was of no further use to me. I'm a woman who craves the exciting friction that only the big stiff masculine peter can yield. I was again driven to tears, such was the extent of my disappointment. I was also enraged beyond repair. My frame quivered not only from passion but also with rage.

George topped this situation by saying in his usual, stoical, English way:

"My word, Miss Flossie, that was a very fine piece of tail . . . yes, it certainly was a good fuck. I still don't think it was right of me to take your cherry."

I controlled my desire to tell that simp that it was I that took his cherry . . . then again, I reckoned, I might not have known his fancies in the art of jazzing. It was possible that I did not appeal to his lustful nature, only his spiritual side. The facts tend vaguely to the latter conclusion.

After he had made the last remark he dismounted me and dressed. I did not talk to him during the time he was clothing himself . . . I was too excited by my inward feelings. I dressed too.

When I arrived at my cabin I found Roland sitting with a disappointed expression on his face. Apparent he was awaiting my return.

"You back so early?" I opened.

"My friend has been confined to his cabin; he had a slight attack of indigestion."

If he had said that his girl friend did not keep her appointment or that she had the monthlies, then I think he would have been speaking the truth—at least his face revealed this assertion. Far be it from me, who was seeped with guilt, to chide him about his disappointment.

I undressed immediately. I was hot . . . a fact that needs no reiteration, and accordinging to my deductions so was he. Roland's lust was rising rapidly as I was undressing. This was lucid to any observer. Apparently my analysis was well founded and true.

After I had completely disrobed, Roland once more noticed my Mons Veneris. It was definitely swollen with unsatisfied desire. I had reclined across the bed and propped my velvety, dimpled knees in a most wanton pose.

I think that all this lewd posing was unnecessary, as Roland was a close second to me in undressing.

"Flossie, you are so temptingly lovely tonight! I am hot for you! See how my prick is nodding to you," he spoke as he stepped out of his last stitch, revealing his far extending tool with its turgid head, ready to complete George's unfinished task.

Oh what a joy for me! I was madly passionate.

"Come, girlie, straddle me," he ordered as he reclined beside me. His prick lashed in the air like a schooner mast in a gale.

I'd have done anything if I knew that it would result in getting his jock locked in my quim. I did as I was directed, while he clung to me kissing and lapping my torso with his burning lips and tongue. Hungrily, my coozie sheathed his gloriously lovable weapon. I melted right down upon it. A prick at last! Not an English imitation of one.

It is needless to stress how I careened and whirled my bottom with Roland's encased dick. My gosh, it was divine! It is difficult to write how I moaned and shouted when I felt the hot blast of his ripe love juices squirting with tremendous force within me. Once was not his limit . . . onward he coaxed, onward I went.

"Wiggle, screw, pump! Oh, Flossie, do anything! Jazz me again and again! Honey, I wish I met you twenty years ago . . . you are the best of the best screws!"

Did I need this urging? I should say most emphatically, no! My own desires were more than equal to his.

I eased my movements for a few moments, after the first come, while I hugged and kissed him with all my jazz-loving soul. Once again I took to the road, twisting my fat, white bottom as my cunnie sucked and pinched his joy-giving dick.

Again and again I spent. Finally I was so weakened by these spasmodic emissions that I could no longer maintain my post. We changed positions.

He continued working his charger in and out. It was all so delicious and satisfying. It certainly was a consoling jazz. Yes, especially after being brutalized by that lazy one-come Englishman whom I now had no further use for; rather, I mean, for his inexperienced prick.

The following day, I noticed that George was very cold toward me. He paid me the same courtesies that he did to any other passenger. There was one passenger though, on whom he lavished his attention extravagantly. She was a surplus hipped, exaggeratedly curved young widow (so I was told)—well, just a tall willowy symmetrically built blonde; her skin was shaded with a coating of olive.

This seductively charming cock-accepter seemed to be deeply fascinated by George's admiration. She strolled the deck gracefully, like a peacock displaying its plumage, posing wantonly whenever George's eyes found her direction.

I know that she was a woman whom every male found desirable, or coveted ... yes, particularly so when the wind would catch her dress and paste it to her Cleopatran torso, lewdly exposing her ass-halves and moulding vividly her more plump-than-mine, men-loved-to-play-with thighs. No doubt, if I were George, I too would have gloated over her form.

As she strolled, her hips shook with snake-like twists, and the avoirdupois of her ass shook like jelly. Unmistakably, she was the type that strongly suggested a most sensuous and hot-fucking jazzer, the kind that knows more ways of twisting a vaginal shaft around a prick than the average veteran whore.

With her aid that evening I learned why George was not content with me, and it was not as I have said, that he was an Englishman.

On that particular evening a ball had been planned; it was our last night at sea. Certainly, I attended this affair. I noticed

George there paying extravagant tribute to this deliciously-cunted blonde.

I awaited an opportunity to eavesdrop on this pair—I was always open to suggestions that would improve my erotic knowledge, for didn't I once say that the only way to hold a man was by catering to his lustful nature?

It was my good fortune to find them seated next to my dining table. I was curious to hear what this striking woman had to say to my one-come-and-finished lover. He called her by the name of Blanche. She was a genuinely prick-hardening picture in the dazzling red, form-clinging gown which she wore that evening. The alluring curves of her bubbie-tops peeped boldly over the top of the daringly low neck. She, if I were to judge by the lustful longing in George's eyes and manners, was the acme of lasciviousness. I strained my ears to hear the gist of their conversation.

"My word, Blanche," he said, fathoming her eyes romantically, "what a wonderful creature you are. You have made me madly passionate for you just looking upon you!"

At this point I had the urge to warn the widow what an empty experience she was to meet with, what an illiterate frigger he actually was. But no one had cautioned me, why should I caution her?

"George, dear," she reacted. "I want you too, but when? Where? You know," she broke off, looking at him through her passion-bedimmed eyes most suggestively.

"I've been teased and fooled," he replied. "I don't mean by that, that I don't understand sentences with unfilled words. I do know what they are supposed to mean but. . . ."

"Don't be silly, dear, you know I want you . . . long for you . . . oh when . . . where can I do it? Where can we be alone? When can we have each other? We want each other . . . don't we?"

"Blanche, my love, I . . . you have made me so happy . . . I'm more certain of myself, so it makes where and when a most simple problem. By jove, I'm excited! You must be wonderful! One of the few that I have met that have appealed to me so strongly . . . and rather upset my senses!

"Meet me in fifteen minutes behind the bridge, and wear a long, dark cloak."

I knew that this meant for her to go to his cabin. While he told her this I observed that he had a most conspicuous hard-on.

I was eager to see what Blanche would do to excite this purser, therefore I followed this desirable and passionate widow. I was determined to know the answers to the information I sought.

When I reached George's cabin I discovered steps which led to the roof. I ascended these silently. I remembered having seen a skylight during my visit to his room. It was via this route that I hoped to enjoy, or rather witness (this is never an enjoyment, to watch couples jazz) the inevitable jazzing scene. I opened this air shaft and slumped down upon my belly to comfortably observe the proceedings below.

Soon the passion-enraged couple entered. In his impatience, George almost tore Blanche's cloak from her sharply defined torso. For a second she posed, statue-like; her eyes glistened with a subtle, amorous stupor. I could see her belly quiver in expectancy. She then yielded to his fervid embrace; soon they were caught in the inescapable nets of the have-to-fuck-you-or-die emotion. She returned his embrace with her flaring lips, while he allowed his hands to glide over her most alluring charms. He removed her titties from their encasement. Two of the most perfectly rounded pieces of human flesh that I have ever seen danced saucily out. Even though I was a woman, I desired to place my mouth over these two appetizing mounds of flesh. There must be many hours of libidinous enjoyment buried in her immaculate white body!

George's tool was very definitely straining his trousers . . . it bulged so that I feared it would rip the buttons from his pants. She felt it and shuddered from the thrilling shock and uttered:

"George, I can't wait . . . please! Shall I undress? Oh, give it to me!"

"Dear, undress of course! Take off everything but your stockings. Egad! Your legs are almost a ravishing dream in those red stockings. I can hardly wait myself!"

First, her red silk gown slipped to the floor then a few other dainties fell, all except her shoes and stockings. I think leaving these garments on tend to make the feminine form more sensuous . . . this rule certainly held good for this case.

I viewed this stark naked woman in wide-eyed amazement. If I was in the same room with her I do not think that I could have resisted her supple form. Boy, what an ass she had . . . spotlessly white, round, more plump than mine, yet firm. I'll bet it even tasted better than the two hot biscuits that the cheeks suggested. Can you blame some women for becoming lesbians? I know I had the urge. What thighs she had! Migosh! Thin at the knees, they tapered evenly as a cone to weld into her gorgeous torso. Between these two pliable cones lay her pussy, poorly protected with a transparent growth of silken hair. Its pouting mouth seemed to emit a vapour that could nourish the most inert peter.

Not only did it seem to do this but also to say: "I am the queen of the clinging-vine pussies. I soothe them, I bottle them up so snugly that there is no surplus space left. Aye, every prick that has ever entered here has never come out alive and I kill them and after they are revived to life they cannot resist the lure to come and be slain again. I am the vampire of cunts!''

Was it my imagination, or did this cunnie in its own particular language express this? In my estimation she had the kind of a nest that men could never over-jazz.

Titties? Oh gee, gosh! Titties! A Greek sculptor could not have done better! Could there have been a more perfect pair than hers? It was seldom that I was awestruck by the feminine form because I found that my form was equal to the best, but Blanche's was many shades closer to the zenith of femininity than mine. I didn't envy her, I admired her as I would anybody who does something outstanding.

I can almost imagine the pleasure that was George's when he dashed those two nice lumps of dainty meat into his mouth. This he did with the zeal of the sacrosanct. Even though his prick was hard and long before he did this, it suddenly became harder and longer. It actually speared from his pubic crop.

Her pussy's mouth was very red, in fact, so much so, that a tinting of lipstick could not have made it more crimson. My guess was that this colour represented her temperament. Scientifically, it doesn't work that way, but what do a bunch of cold, calculating scientists know about an honest to goodness fuck. I'll bet George burned his prick as he rammed it into those two smiling lips.

Let's go through the scene more systematically. George quickly undressed, dropped to his knees then clasped her thighs and ass. He buried his face in the profusion of silky curls beneath her rippling belly. She must have screamed . . . she might have even shrieked, because I heard her utterance above the roar of the boat's whistle.

"George! George, don't kiss me there! Wait until I can kiss you at the same time. Oh gawd I'm hot!"

She was as she stated, broiling in the vent.

With feline grace she crept upon the bed; a silent, lewd, inviting smile formed upon her lips as she propped her artistic thighs upward, at the same time parting them. Thus the fullness of her cunnie was revealed to my eyes for the first time. What a beautiful cunnie it was! Full, round, firm meaty lips!

"Come and enjoy me, I am yours . . . all yours. Do your will!"

It didn't take George long to accept the invitation, and I would have done the same, had I been in a convenient position to do so, woman though I was. I still cannot understand why these two lips appealed to me so strongly.

I heard distinctly every one of their love maddened cries, grunts and moans. I could honestly appreciate their fantastically excited emotions. What a glory must have been theirs. In my humble opinion no greater one can be had.

This scene was a superlatively exciting one. Indeed, I can hardly write it properly because the highlights race through my mind and reach my paper before events that have happened before these. There was a preliminary exercise before George entered; I have not overlooked mentioning it but as I think of that scene my mind whirls with the desires for the male stiff and I cannot seem to concentrate.

When Blanche first sprawled upon the bed, George reclined beside her and felt the alluring widow from cunnie to tits. She reciprocated by playing with his rampant tool, ever cautious not to bring it to the point of spending.

Apparently Blanche was an experienced wanton. She seemed to know exactly how long she should engage in such preliminaries.

Since she had her fill of warming up the cunt exercises, she did something which to this very day, I have not seen equalled. Slowly, in a lascivious manner, she spread her legs. I could see her crimson-hued pussy staring through her blonde curls. First it lengthened then broadened, as she continued to open her mellow thighs. Gosh, she must have had power over her cunnie muscles! It reminded me of an operator controlling marionettes. Her magnetic thighs continued to arc until she revealed a delicious looking, puffed lipped, deep red gash . . . the flower had completely opened its bud into full bloom; this is my best analogy. Her pussy seemed to have opened its mouth to take a bite of a delicious meal. The lips quavered rapidly with an enormous appetite for George's bursting cock.

George found her clitty with his lips. He must have done this with delicate masterfulness for it warranted from her a sudden upward thrust of her bottom while stifling moans escaped from her throat.

"You dear boy . . . not yet darling . . . how lovely it feels! No . . . oh, no! Please! You will make me . . . come on quick, put it in . . . Fuck me! Oh please fuck!" Her voice sank to a whisper as she broke from speaking.

Gee, she looked frantic! How George worked his mouth on her clitty! It must have felt truly divine. Evidently he enjoyed kissing and lapping her quim, because he did not ease his operation in that dangerously sensitive territory.

He continued moving his head, playing his tongue more deeply into her cock-loving slit. Her audible and heavy breathing was an unmistakable sign of the tremendous amount of pleasure that she was receiving.

This was not all that I had to judge from. Her crisis came. She moved about like a chicken with its head chopped off, kicking, heaving, crying, praying and whatnot. I never have seen any person undergo such contorted movements during the act of spending. If the amount of moving and screaming during a spend can be used to determine the amount of pleasure the victim receives I should say that she was experiencing one of the most delicious and exaggerated spends that I have ever witnessed.

Her writing was so different and markedly acute that I have little trouble in recalling it my mind. Why couldn't I enjoy such a luxurious spend?

After she had recovered, having been satisfied with the way he executed that antecedent, George arose.

Her semi-closed eyes gloated over his palpitating wand with a fanatical eagerness.

"Oh," she whimpered in a pant, "put . . . shove . . . stab me with your beauty with all your might . . . shove it hard! Rip me open! I'm insane for it! Tear me to pieces with it if you will!"

With such delirious pleas who would hesitate? Not George. He lost no time in lunging his purple-knobbed dick into the hilt. Boy! I'll bet that felt good! Then the most erotic and vuloptuous surrender to lustful endeavours that I have ever seen began. I was actually fascinated by their technique, particularly Blanche's elastic movements. The way which she prevented him from coming a second time so that she could obtain another spend was nothing short of remarkable.

After many minutes—or was it hours?—of poignantly blissful jazzing they slumped motionless into each other's entwining arms. They sealed their lips and exchanged an ever so intoxicating kiss. This seemed to inflame both to the point of eagerness for another feast.

Blanche once more surrendered herself to her wildest desires. Violently she rolled, shook and quivered. Wantonly, she wound a long slender calf plus a plump conical thigh around his back . . . gee, but this made me hot! Then she locked her feet, holding George at her mercy; she drew him closer to her wide-open slit. She undulated her belly with more rapid motions than a frightened eel. Boy! Oh boy! How she could roll her ass around! And in such perfect accordance with her lover's strokes.

Plainly I could see how her pussy swallowed his oversized rod and how his steaming cock beat a rapid passage in and out. I could even hear the smacking of her cunt's lips as they embraced the charging cock.

Both were maudlin with lustful sensations, screwing like mad each time a spend convulsed them. Slowly their delirium to jazz themselves to death subsided. They reposed in a blissful die-away.

Blanche arose and dressed. Before she had

completed her toilette George's peter had primed itself and was ready for another round. He sat on a chair as his joint lurched wildly in the air.

"Oh, Blanche, I have just a small bit left . . . take it before you leave!"

Noticing what he meant as she turned abut, she returned. "You dear generous boy . . . how I love it!"

She raised her red dress most anxiously. Ah, again she had exposed to my view her most delectable fucking machine. It was beautiful from the colour it had gained from such strained use. With her fuckable hips exposed in this manner she walked over to where George was sitting and straddled his monster. This was a position new to me, and naturally I wanted to try it at the next available opportunity. She rapidly sheathed the purser's rampant tool.

Then the Fourth of July had begun again! This gorgeous jazzable girl pranced and pumped her bottom around in spite of George's tight hold upon it. Both tipped their heads backwards and rolled their eyes crazily. When the ecstatic melting point of passion was reached I heard Blanche scream, and then slump forward, motionless. Apparently she had fainted.

If she did I can readily imagine the cause . . . the intense pleasure was too much for her conscious mind. Funny, isn't it? We faint when we are overcome by pain and we faint when we are overcome by pleasure.

In the meantime George was gasping and pushing his ass upwards so that he could drain every drop from his overworked balls. It was exactly this kind of an experience that I needed yesterday when I was with George. Now I see why he failed to deliver it. It was entirely my fault.

This tempestuous bout had made me extremely desirous to engage in an unrelentless and torrid screwing. Nothing short of what I had seen would satisfy me in the condition that I was then in.

I hurried down from my perch and to my cabin; my cunt left a hot trail of air as I ran. That's how hot I was! I made my goal but I was close to the point of exhaustion when I reached it . . . of course not from running, from my maniacal desire to be prick-pierced.

Seeing a person get well-fucked is enough to set any normal person on fire but I am by far more sensitive at my titties and clitty than most people, therefore you can try to imagine how sorely I was in need of Roland's joy-rod.

My lover was sleeping when I entered the compartment. I was too damn cock-crazy to care, I merely woke him up. I told him what had happened. I played with his balls and cock, as I tried to vividly describe the scene which I had just witnessed. By the time I neared the end of my tale, Roland substituted his interest for what I was telling him, to a more dominating one—putting his tool between the meshy folds of my pulsating, anxious flesh. His instrument too, was bobbing with impatience. Heavens! Now we were both mad with lustful wants!

Few seconds were lost in Roland's mounting me. Yesterday I knocked George for disregarding preliminaries, today I would have cursed Roland for regarding such introductory exercises. I certainly am inconsistent . . . I guess that's one of the many things that are titled under: women's special privileges!

To the balls Roland buried his joint. Oh, boy! It felt good as it tore past my clitty, lips and cervix. Its pliant head singed and thrilled as it rode into my mellow folds of flesh. How tightly my cunnie lips hugged his entering prick. How I hoped that he could insert his balls and more! He wallowed in my lustful hole but did not come until I had three supinely lustful spends . . . and they were lustful! Why, I came all over the pillow that was propping my cunnie section up to meet his charger more securely. Come? Huh, that was nothing—why I drenched his balls and his pubic beard. Gee, I came! I thought that my stomach would gush out with my dew. Damn, how I loved and enjoyed it!

Finally he cried and whimpered as a forewarning, then his jets opened to release his intoxicating streams of creamy juice which mixed with the generous supply of my love liquor. We were then both submerged by the fantastic pleasures of spewing inebriation.

Drunk from the effects of gratified lust, with his cock in my roost, we fell into a dreamy sleep.

At the dawn of the new morning we found ourselves in London.

5

5

We remained in London long enough to meet Roland's son, Carl, who accompanied us to Paris.

Carl was a handsome youth, genteel and mannered. He was the image of his dad in every way . . . perhaps a bit more handsome. He appeared to be an ideal specimen of virile, muscular manhood. I had at that time supposed that he had inherited his dad's loving nature.

An indescribable magnetic attraction was held for me in those two jet-black eyes of his . . . somehow they fascinated me.

"What a wonderful prick he must have," I thought and as I did, I breathed a long passionate sigh.

Judging by these circumstances, one does not have to wonder long to conclude that after a short time had passed I found myself deeply interested in Carl—too interested.

With a sly wink in his eye, Roland introduced me to his son as his adopted American daughter. Seemingly, that is to me, to understand his father's customs perfectly, Carl breathed an understanding of my status. He demonstrated this understanding because he never showed any other desire for relationship with me other than friendliness. He was most congenial and respectful to me.

In Paris, Carl helped us to settle and refurnish the apartment. There I was promoted to the ranks of a veritable queen. I entertained Roland's many friends lavishly.

Carl's continued indifference toward my charms had a most peculiar and teasing effect upon my cunnie. He seemed bashful. He must have been, gracious me, but I showed him every type of encouragement that I knew. The only thing that remained for me to do was to take my pussy out and serve it to him on a golden platter.

What can a girl do who tries to lead a fellow, by discreet diplomacy, into a cock-in-the-cunt conversation and he skilfully or naïvely evades the issue each time. Is it possible that he really thought I was his father's adopted daughter? I didn't think so!

I wanted him to jazz me; yes, very, very much indeed! I couldn't be so indecent as to ask him bluntly nor could I pick up my dress, lie on the floor, prop my knees up and throw my legs far apart and say, come, come dear, fuck me. No, that would never do. What kind of a girl would he think I was? A good-for-nothing whore, whom his dad must rid himself of.

I liked Carl for his apparent respect for me ... yet I didn't like him for the very reason that I did like him. It sounds quite unbalanced but I was torn between these two feeling: liking him because he respected me and hating him because he would not sink his tool into my quim. Was I crazy? I'll say I was ... about Carl.

I was not in Paris very long when I observed that the average girl wore dresses to and above her knees. Their stockings were rolled below the knees, revealing the dimpled fullness of those charms. Shapely calves were plentiful, but none were as symmetrical as mine ... or so I thought. After all, this was my favourite way of wearing my socks ... it was the vogue ... one habit that I wouldn't have to change.

To me it appeared as though few of the truly seductively shaped women wore slips and some neglected tit-holders. The sun readily sifted through their gowns, freely exposing the exact shape of their thighs until they reached their cunts.

The Parisians seemed to have a fondness for displaying large titties. This they did, as I have already mentioned, by not patronizing the brassiere shops. Those that did wear bub-prisoners wore the type that only braces the bottom of them and makes the outline of the tips point saucily out of the dress.

With these features already in mind we can see how enticing the average French miss looked. They weren't satisfied to look just merely as enticing as their clothes would permit them to look, oh no. Each woman had cultivated a lewd walk. This had a most arousing effect upon the men, and one could almost tell by their walk what kind of movement they used when they jazzed. They all daringly suggested many long hours of lustful entities.

As the time passed Carl did not add to the amount of attention that he was paying me. He still paid the same amount of heed that courtesy demanded. This situation did begin to change. Perhaps it was after I had overheard this conversation:

"Son, why are you so cool to Flossie? You know your dad has no objections to your being more friendly and intimate with her. Go to it, son!" he finished, slapping him good-naturedly on the back.

Carl did show a slightly changed attitude from that day on; I couldn't appreciate the change though. How could I? There was no fucking as a result. Even after the encouragement that Roland gave him, Carl was still shy. It took him over a month before he would get near enough to me to put his arm around me. I began to wonder whether he was a queer. If he wasn't one he certainly had his maidenhead.

"Carl," I asked one day, "why are you such a woman-hater?"

"I'm not."

"You certainly act like it. How come you don't go out with them oftener than you do?"

"Women rather tire me. They're sort of boring . . . they all talk about one thing."

"And what is that?" I popped.

"Aw . . . dresses and such nonsense."

"Oh," I sighed, surprised and disappointed by his remark, "is that all?"

"Isn't that boring enough? I didn't learn styles when I went to college. After all, you know I took engineering as applied to the shipbuilding industry."

"Why, Carl, it's absurd to think that women should even think of discussing such a topic. You don't expect them to, do you?"

"Of course not, but when they change the topic of style and all that bosh, they usually talk about filth."

I was going to say that they should do it rather than talk about it but I think it was my good fortune not to have done so.

"And when they tire of wagging their tongues about dirty things then they want to pet and kiss, you know. No good ever comes out of being left unsatisfied by just the beginning of a sexual relation . . . a kiss is to a sexual relation what an appetizer is to a meal: both leave you desiring more. If you have ever been real hungry and a large Porterhouse steak has been set in front of

131

you, but you're only allowed a small portion of it—it's maddening—see what I'm driving at?"

"I think so ... just this: petting causes one to become hungry sexually, a good dish causes one to become hungry gastronomically. In other words, a person would be better off if he wouldn't pet unless the whole sexual meal was a part of the diet. Right?" I looked up at him and smiled triumphantly.

"Perfectly correct! Very well stated."

Since I found the cause of Carl's shyness perhaps I could handle him to fit into my plans, I thought ... but then, couldn't he have used that lengthy explanation for a protective measure, to cover up an inferiority complex? I did not know exactly which way to render my decision. I guess I leaned in the direction in which I could benefit mostly.

It often happens when people are timid towards some type of attainment, or any problem that they think they cannot conquer, they build a philosophy to show why that object which they are afraid to attempt to overcome is not desirable.

This self-constructed argument shields their timidity. Did Carl speak the truth or did he have an inferiority complex in reference to jazzing? Hard as it might be to believe, it still was possible.

If what he had said were the truth, then few people would pet unless they knew positively that their efforts were going to end with a sealing of the prick in the cunt. It is hard to believe this last assertion; look about you and you will readily find the truth supplied.

Ordinary means, I decided, would not compel Carl to shed a drop of his cream. I began to let different schemes and plans race through my mind by which I might rob him of his generous supply. I needed a third party to assist me with this task. I picked my maid to play the part in this potential plot. Before she would be of any further use to me, she must qualify as any actress would in the attempt to gain a role. First I had to be sure that I could trust her implicitly.

As a rule I wore silks from my stockings to my scandalously short dresses. Roland was more than pleased to see me dress this way. About two months after my arrival I was being assisted into a new, very spicy costume by my maid.

My maid was a very chic young French girl, a few years older than myself but many years my senior in sexual knowledge. Her eyes and hair were raven black ... both contained a lustrous sparkle. Like most French girls, she had a doll-like face, wide voluptuous lips and a pair of milky white bubbies, slightly larger than the average well-formed size; anyway they looked darned good to me. Most normal men like this kind for the purpose of burying their meat sticks between them and painting them with a luscious coating of their creamy white spew, making them even more tasy and desirable.

From her, I not only learned the fine points of dress, but also many excellent hints that improved the movements of my prick-hugging cunnie. Generously she donated to me from her vast fund of sexual knowledge; new positions, how to more minutely control my pussy and other facts that would fill a chapter.

This day she insisted upon giving me a bath. I thought that it would be thrilling to be sponged all over by a woman, and even if it might not be I thought I should try it just to gain that new experience. Somehow when one views my nude body I feel a peculiar heat seeping into my veins and cunnie.

"Ooo-la-la!" Maybelle, my maid, chanted as she bathed me, concentrating her attention on my cunnie and titties, "zee Mees Flossie, as, she ees vair'ee beautiful . . . such a nice form, you know? Voluptuous, how you Amair'can's say eet? Monsieur Carl, he weel go craizy when he sees you . . . what you say it? Bubbies. They air, madam, zee finest pair een all Paree!"

"Why do you mention Carl?" I asked in anticipation of hearing in her reply some complimentary or encouraging remark made to her by Roland's handsome son concerning me.

"Ah, Carl, he ees one zat like zee preety

girl . . . he ees some galantee!" She rolled
her eyes and shook her generous hips and
bubbies.

Even though I was curious to know
whether she had ever been with Carl, I
refrained from asking her . . . that would be
poor diplomacy. Women as a rule do not
answer those questions, when asked point
blank, truthfully. I suppressed my question.

She continued bathing me, chatting in her
quaint dialect of English spoken with French
accents. At each limb she would pause and
comment, but when she reached my hairy
nest, she almost went into spasms of glee.

"Oo-la-la, mmm, what a pretty birdie you
have!" she exclaimed as she clasped her
hand over my slit and pressed the hot flesh
firmly.

There was an intangible quality in her
mannerism that made me feel hot. It might
have been her deliberate lewdness.

"Oh! No! No! No! Everything ees right,
here een Paree!" she encouraged. "Eet ees
stylish for you to have a young lovair . . .
evairy Amair'can girl has one!"

It was at this point in our conversation
that I began to realize that she would make
an excellent confidant. Her broad views and
ideals were very similar to mine. There was
no reason why I shouldn't cultivate a more
intimate relationship with her. And then
there was her knowledge of the handling of
men; I felt sure that it was superior to mine.

Perhaps she could help me steer Carl's jock into my cunnie. I marked these notes indelibly in my mind ... excellent for future reference, I thought.

That afternoon, I was sitting in my boudoir, toying with my hair and features as I sipped some cordial. Carl entered, a shade more gay and jovial than it was his custom. Naturally I was startled; never before had he entered my boudoir and even at that he had never seen me with so few clothes on. I blushed at his sudden approach. I do not know why, exactly ... it happened though. My mirror told that tale.

I looked up at him in wide-eyed amazement (Was I returning to modesty again?) and uttered:

"Carl, what are you doing here ... what will your father say?"

I think his sudden appearance bewildered me so that I said things that the average woman would say instinctively. I certainly didn't mean what I said. It seems like I have always done and said things that I have repented for afterwards ... what causes it, some subconscious inner voice?

Carl, uncertain of his footing, wheeled about the room without replying. He smiled and then spoke:

"Floshie, dad, he ain't here ick, don't mind me, ick, Maybelle and I were out this

afternoon . . . just had a little too much, ick
. . . got a little hick-ick-cups."

"Carl, I'm surprised! You drunk! How did
you get that way? Where have you been?"

"Lishen, honey, I know what I'm saying
. . . I ain't too drunk, ick."

It was plain to see that he was exerting
himself to hold his feet steady. Then a
sudden thought came over me: I could fuck
him! A real solution to my demands. Did
Maybelle do this for me because she could
read my mind? She must have because she
asked me many times where I would be all
that day. She was a dear!

"Where is Maybelle? She might get hurt,
alone and drunk."

"Ick, she's all right . . . she said she would
meet me here and I should go right home.
Were you waiting for me like she said you
would? Maybelle said, ick, I should come
home and play with your, ah, birdie . . . I
don't shee no, ick, birdie.

"Shay, Floshie, you sure have a pretty leg,
ick . . . I wanna kish it."

As best he could he slumped to his knees;
first he kissed my hand and after letting his
eyes sway over my soft pink knees he kissed
them passionately on the dimples. In spite
of his semi-conscious state he did this with
tact, first one then the other. I didn't think
a person who is inebriated could appreciate
the charms of a woman.

"How   mm-mmm-charming!   How

tempting!" he spoke in a coarse whisper, panting. I didn't know whether he was panting from passion or from wines.

I was beginning to recover from my shock. I was getting control of my senses and I began to realize there was a golden opportunity knocking at my coozie door. I was going to get Carl's prick if I had to take it while he was drunk! I didn't know how to react towards him so I played him as though he was sober.

"Oh, Carl!" I spoke excitedly, like a child getting something she had cried her eyes out for. "Why do you kiss me there?" Then I made my voice almost inaudible as I finished, "when there is something so much nicer further up?"

I think he heard me because he flushed; I did, I know.

"I kish you there because I like you . . . Maybelle told me I did . . . shay can I give you a French, ick, kish?"

"What kind of a kiss is that?" I lied, innocently. If he wasn't as drunk as he seemed I would be playing my game safely.

"I'll show you."

"Are you sure it isn't naughty?"

"Why, Floshie, how can you shay shuch things? It's so nice you'll just love it to death."

He grabbed me by the bottom, his eyes flashed a youthful vigour and he sank his face between my lovely thighs. There were no panties there to hinder his project. Gosh, how I wilted when his hot breath fanned my box! How I melted when his burning lips sank into the pulpy fold of my crack. I closed my eyes and wallowed in the bliss of his passionate outburst. The way he began to make love made me think that he was putting on a drunken act to gain admittance to my privates ... or, did he have to get drunk before he could make love? More problems, but who worries about those things when they are hot in the box? I don't; all I think about then is: how long will it be before he rams it in?

He picked his face out of my dewing slit and smiled at me crazily:

"I wonder what dad would do if he caught me Frenching his daughter?"

"Don't think of such things, Carl, dear! We must be very careful ... when you are more sober we can have some nice times together. Do you like me a little, Carl ... just a little bit?"

"Floshie, I love you ... I loved you as shoon as I walked into this room ... drunk or not drunk, ick, I love you. I'm just wild about kishing your beautiful legs and I guess you know what that means. Did you know that my dad loves beautiful young girls like you too, ick. My dad and me, ick, are pals. We love our women pretty and voluptuoush like you, Floshie, ick."

He began to run his hand around my fat

bottom, up and down the crack. It felt so soothing and good. I wasn't comfortable because I was seated on a backless boudoir chair so I led him over to the bed where we both reclined.

"Thish is shwell, just like I shee in the movies . . . I'll bet you ish going to, ick, love me."

"Carl, don't be so silly . . . snap out of it . . . please, can't you see that I want you!"

"You want me . . . here I am . . . what do, ick, you want me for?"

"Lay back, dearest . . . that's a nice boy."

"Ah, thish ish shwell."

Suddenly as though he had become sobered he lifted up my negligee and gloated over my quim.

"Gee, Floshie, it's cute! Shay, ick it's schwell! You don't mind if I look at it."

I grasped his dummy in my hand to see whether all this treatment had any effect upon him. My gosh! It was so hard I was afraid that it would pop if I didn't hustle it in my quim. I really became alarmed!

He began to make love to me in a fitful way. Even in his drunkness I was fascinated by his methods. He, rather I, removed his clothing to give him the freedom that lovemaking requires. I also removed my few pieces of scanties.

He parted my legs and placed one of mine in the solid vice of his and squeezed it. Then, holding me firmly that way, he allowed his fingers to delicately play with my fleshy lips. He nipped and pinched the sensitive folds most affectionately. It excited my vulval region to a fucking temperature.

Nude as I was, his hands found no obstacles to interfere with his progress and wanton explorations around my fat bottom and silken-haired crack. I returned his entreaties by fondling his velvety-headed prick, running my fingers around the ring and meshing its soft plushy eye.

I was becoming more passionate all the while. I hoped Carl knew what he was doing; I harboured a vague fear that he might heat me to a maddening temperature and then leave me to suffer in my agony . . . but where is the man who is hotter than all the fires of hell who loves a woman and then leaves her without crowning the occasion with a lecherous jazz? It might have been done but I have never heard of it. Which man wants a nut-ache that bad?

Carl's lips were very warm . . . torrid, would be more correct. I suppose the heat was partially due to his intoxicated condition. I still think that my quim was hotter. We kissed and played with each other for perhaps a half hour and still he made no suggestion of mounting the road to ecstatic bliss.

Gosh, I was so damned passionate my cunt itched all the way up to my hardened bubbies. My whole insides burned with lustful needs . . . would he ever put it in?

"Oh, Carl," I cried out after I could retain my speech no longer, "you are mean to torment me this way. Oh if you won't put it in . . . kiss it with all your might! Don't stop, till . . . till . . . I . . . I . . . oh . . . Carl, how lovely?" I exclaimed as I felt the full force of the kiss which he had planted deeply between my legs on my quivering, pouting pussy.

This worked me to such a state of erotic fury that I spent and he was only tickling my clitty with his tongue. I almost screamed from the lovely sensations.

I sputtered in delirium:

"Oh, Carl . . . how I love it! Here . . . here . . . here it comes! There! Feel it squeeze! Oh, Carl, dear . . . your tongue . . . in . . . put it way in . . . ooo-ah! how delicious!"

His hands were squeezing my fat bottom, then he reached up and moulded my bubs. Was this all? I still wanted his prick . . . nothing short of that could satisfy me now.

"Suck it, Carl! Eat it! oh . . . aaahhssssuh! Suck it! You . . . you darling boy!" I moaned and gasped as I melted and spent again.

My very soul seemed to ooze out of my womb as I heard and felt the lapping, sucking, and licking sounds of his tongue as he hungrily extracted the essences of my love. His eyes were limpid and sparkling with lustful satisfaction as he gazed at my swollen and inflamed quim.

Of course, my readers will say: "Why did she allow him to only lap her?" I will explain.

Carl was drunk . . . to me it seemed as though he was only faintly aware of what he was doing. I wanted him to jazz me in the normal way . . . ten times if he could! That's how hot I was! But to be fucked by he who is drunk is a rather hard task, unless they themselves takes the initiative. A drunk always uses his will and as you know is almost numb to suggestions.

My other reason: if Carl wasn't as drunk as I thought he was, I wanted to break the chaste relationship between us as meekly as possible. He previously demonstrated the fact that he was either shy or timid. If I urged him to things other than his natural inclinations then he might have withdrawn entirely. And if he wasn't as drunk as I thought he was then he would remember that he had had a sexual meal with me and I would be able to conquer his prick so much more easily and satisfactorily in his more sober moments.

It was my plan to reach an understanding with him, to arrange for a night of voluptuous pleasures, a night when we could both be naked and free from any cares. Roland could have walked in any minute.

When Carl had finished he stood up trembling and panting. I helped him into his clothes. He was really becoming harder to handle. His manly rod was still rigid, for it bulged his trousers very noticeably. One consoling fact, I learned, it was much larger than his dad's.

"Floshie," he said, half-dazed, "you was shwell, you owe me something?"

"What, dearest?" I looked into his lazy eyes and straightened his mussed hair.

"Yeah, ick, you owe me a French kish, I gave you one . . . you should pay me back right away . . . here it ish big," he said drowsily as he flourished the biggest prick I ever saw.

Oh, gee, gosh! It certainly looked good to me! It looked to me to be as large as that cop's club over at 42nd and Broadway back in the States.

Here was the handsomest cock that I had ever seen before me, big, turgid, meaty . . . why didn't I notice it before while I was playing with it? Now, after the show was over I noticed what I had overlooked. What a head it had, most ideally shaped for exciting use and beautifully coloured; purple and glossy, tapering widely to a heavy-knobbed club point. The broad crimson collar was covered with minute thorny substances. The long, perfectly formed shaft was clothed with the whitest, cleanest and plushiest skin, moulded firmly to his cock, like bark on a tree. A pair of large, but firm balls to match his cock in size and beauty completed his loving equipment. All this machinery rose majestically from a thick tuft of curly hair.

The beauty in my hand was hard and horny. I could not dent it with my firm grip. It was so strongly attached to his belly that I could hardly budge it up and down. When I did so it would snap back with a loud and resounding thud against his stomach. So powerful a tool could only belong to a youth of tremendous vigour and unconquerable vitality. What man wouldn't be proud to possess such an immaculate weapon? And what woman wouldn't be proud and thrilled to spheres beyond recounting to have been the recipient of such a gorgeous dick.

I wondered if I could open my mouth wide enough to get this wonderful organ in it. I couldn't find out unless I tried.

Before I did so these words flowed right out of my mouth:

"Carl, how handsome it is; I'm in love with it!"

I had hoped that he would understand and appreciate the full significance of my remark.

"Dash what all the women shay. Shuck on it, it won't bite you . . . shee it shoot."

I began to lead this colossal cock towards my mouth and Carl blurted again in his insobriety:

"Wash out, Floshie, it might shoot in your

face and knock one of, ick, ick, your eyes out . . . you're too nish a girl . . . shay, how much you going to charge me?"

I could only listen to his babbling because I was trying to gurgle his prick down my throat.

I did manage to squeeze, "Mmm . . . how lovely . . . I'll . . . I . . . mmmuhh," past his choking but delicious tool.

"Floshie, I ain't going to give more unk . . ." and he seemed to forget to finish the sentence. He was growing more intoxicated all the time. I sat him down and continued my work.

"Ah, feels good, Floshie . . . feels good! Feels like a cat's tongue."

I again slipped the head between my teeth and wound my tongue about the head. Boy, oh boy! It sure tasted good! It was so hot that it singed my mouth. The plushy head was so soothing in my mouth—I could suck it forever.

"At's the girlie, chew it, shuck it harder . . . feels sho good. Shay, make . . . make me come . . . what do you think thish ish? What do you think I'm paying . . ." and his head dropped to his chest.

His desire for more action was shown by his weakly moving in and out. Once in a while he gave a grunt for pleasure, and shoved with more force, almost bottling up my throat with it. He trembled and shook all over, most of the time clutching his balls with one hand. I assumed that his placing his hands over his balls was a hint for me to do that for him; I took the hint. I could feel the virile liquid moving about in his stone-like bag.

"My gosh! Floshie, honey, be careful you ish going to make me come in your mouth . . . if you do it will feel sho good in your belly, but you will get drowned . . . you can shwim, huh, Floshie?"

When he said this I thought he was nearing the spewing point so I hastened my actions. My neck was beginning to get stiff. I believe that I had been working about thirty-five minutes and I was beginning to feel that I merited a rich creamy come for my untiring efforts.

Carl was beginning to doze and grow non-chalant. I caressed the sensitive nerve centres under the head in my efforts to make it come more quickly. I did everything that I could to hasten the spew but my efforts were in vain. I was continually growing more eager for his dew. I loved the boy; I wanted to drink his love potion.

Beads of sweat had long ago formed on my forehead. My entire body was coated with a heavy layer of perspiration. Gee-zoo, I was working! I think my cunnie was as hot inside as my body was outside and the only thing that could soothe me was a generous dose from his love faucets. It seemed as though he was already sleeping, but that did not tend to discourage me. A person can come in their sleep. I sucked more frantically as the time passed; my neck felt like it was breaking. Who pauses to regard a breaking neck when they are lust enraged? Not I. The thought that someone might enter and interfere with my much coveted come passed through my mind; that only made me labour more furiously. At times I felt like I was swooning and then again I thought, if this dick was only in my cunt what a jazz it would make. I knew that was impossible . . . he was already too drunk to support himself on his hands and knees. I determined that if no one interrupted I was going to suck until he came . . . even if it took all night.

I squeezed his balls, jerked his foreskin over the head, and yet there was no come. His balls remained hard as rocks, inflated almost to the point of bursting. This meant that there was enough fluid in them to support a discharge. Saliva was running all over his trousers—these I kept up and buttoned with the exception of those that had to be left open so that his prick and balls could come through. This I did so that in the event that someone entered I could hastily show an innocent front.

I was beginning to give up in despair when I heard someone walking in the corridor outside our apartment. As I was expecting Roland, I thought it was he, and I began to withdraw my mouth from his balls when I felt them begin to squeeze and shrink toward his staff. Was he at the coming point and was Roland to catch me amid this straining, but highly delectable act? When I heard the footsteps pass my apartment I gave a tremendous sigh of relief and plunged his prick once more into my mouth. Damn it! And it was at the coming point when I left.

All this time Carl was fast asleep in a drunken stupour. The only reason I continued to pump his love-well for some cream was because I had heard that men come in their sleep when they have wet dreams. Was drunkenness any different from sleep? Yes, I learned the difference several months after this event. At this time and until I was told otherwise, I thought that Carl was just a natural late-comer. I now know the best way for a woman to work her coozie dry is to jazz a drunk; sometimes they come and sometimes they don't. If they do it usually takes over an hour. I should have realized that because I had already sucked on Carl's honey for a longer time than that.

My brain was beginning to numb; so was my neck and back. Diligently I stuck to my task; I was either going to make him come or die in the attempt. I can't understand to this very day why I had wanted to run such a perilous risk. If I wanted spew there were plenty of men who would have readily made that sacrifice.

I tried every motion that I knew with my tongue and mouth but to no advantage. It seemed as though I was still where I had begun, only I was dangerously panting and urging myself onward. I knew he had to come—every man has to sooner or later. I adhered to my work like one who is drowning clutches any object that he might find safety upon. Desperately, my heart thundering, my lungs expanding, with my jaws paralysed to his sweet meat I still clamoured for my much merited reward—a hot, forceful, thick, creamy spend. I was blindly determined to get it at any cost!

My cunnie was burning hot and the spew I so dearly coveted would have gushed down my throat and cooled that sizzling organ. Occasionally I would bury my finger between my meshy, torrid lips and try to cool it that way. I came once as a result—not a very healthy spend.

After working about twenty minutes longer I felt his balls begin to tug and shrink. At last he was going to shoot! I worked more desperately . . . my senses were growing dim, my instincts seemed to lead me on. His prick-head began to swell in my mouth. Like a big bubble it continued to inflate. Numbed as my body was, with the exception of my itching coozie and my mouth, I sensed the approach of this blissful occasion. I was hardly conscious of my neck and mouth moving rapidly—I know it was—but my body seemed to be moving automatically. Dimly, I began to realize the bliss that would soon be mine.

My hand was still weakly clutching his ever hardening balls. I knew that any second a boiling stream of precious dew would be bombarding my mouth and throat. Aware of the fact that I was nearing the acme of zest I threw every fragment of my surplus but dying energy into my movements. My brain whirled, my tongue cleaved mightily to his swelling prick-head, my heart thundered in anxiety from my toils; my pussy throbbed and itched in accordance with my excited state.

His prick began to tighten! His belly sucked it inwards, then suddenly it released and I felt a hot stream of terrific force gush its way down my parching-for-spew throat, then I felt a rapid succession of bobs; each bob released another river of honeyed cream.

I know I wasn't conscious when this was happening. I felt like I was either dreaming or in a daze. I could feel my mouth unrelentlessly sucking his prick as it surrendered its precious cargo. Everything then became black.

When I awoke I found myself lying in bed clad in a pair of silk pyjamas, a pair that I hadn't worn before! I was in my room. I looked about very puzzled. Was it a dream? Where was Carl? There was not a single bit of evidence that he had been there. I know that no one other than myself could have put me to bed although Roland might have done so. Maybelle had her afternoon off.

I tried to arise from bed; I realised it couldn't possibly have been my imagination. I couldn't get up. My neck, back, and every other part of my once subtle body was paralysed. I couldn't have gotten that stiff sleeping as a bedmate to Rip Van Winkle. I didn't try any longer to arise but fell into a dream-filled sleep in which Carl was the dreamed of, in every sexual embrace I knew of and some that I didn't.

At about six o'clock that evening Maybelle awoke me. She carried a tray with supper. I was still tired and did not feel at all like getting out of bed.

How I got in bed and dressed puzzled me; what happened to Carl was another problem. I looked at my maid, trying to see whether there were hidden secrets within her eyes. She wore a most unconcerned expression.

"Suppair, Meess Flossie."

"Thank you."

"Why do you lay een bed . . . don't you feel well?" she said, with a bright twinkle in her eyes.

"I don't know . . . just plain lazy . . . maybe tired."

Why should she ask me why I was in bed? Many a time I ate supper in my boudoir and she never made a remark. I began to suspect her. It then dawned upon me that Carl said that he had been with her before he came up. She knew much more than she was willing to admit.

"Oh, Maybelle," I called as she stepped out of the room, "come here, I want to ask you something."

"What ees eet that I can do for you?"

"Have you seen Carl this afternoon?"

"Yes."

"Have you seen Roland?"

"No."

"Why are you smiling, Maybelle? Come, come . . . is it a secret to keep from Roland?"

"Yes . . . you leetle devil . . . you naughty naughty girl . . . you fall to sleep on zee job, yes?"

"Thánk goodness it was you . . . you put me to bed? What happened to Carl?"

"Oh, I get zee elevatair man, he helped me with heem . . . he ees steell dronk, zee peeg! We put heem een hees room. Now don't worry, evairytheeng weell be O.K. . . . ees zat zee way you Amair'cans say eet?"

"I could hug you to death for this . . . you're a dear!"

"Did he do eet to you . . . you loved eet?"

"No, not in the way you mean."

"No . . . oh eet ees so wonderful! I had eet

153

before he came to see you . . . some preek he has? How he can jazz!"

"Maybelle, I envy you. You make me hot by talking about it . . . mmm, such a great big one!"

"You had bettair not do any jazzing until tomorrow, you air much too tired."

"I am, but my cunnie never is."

"You leetle devil . . . you and I ees see same, my body get terribly tired but my birdie she nevair want a rest."

At that my maid cupped her hand over my cunnie. Then she drew off the bedclothes and lifted my negligee. This made me extremeley hot. Anyone would have wanted to screw if they had seen that lustful shine in those two beaming, anxious black eyes of Maybelle. My clitty became rigid, my lips puffed and everything about me was in readiness to fuck . . . but the prick was lacking.

"Please, please don't, Maybelle . . . it feels so nice, yet it will only leave me . . . oh you know!"

"Meess Flossie, I weell nevair leave you; no, no, no, not that way. I weel feex you up nice. Yes?"

She then began to churn my clitty with her index finger. She also swabbed my slit between the meaty lips with her other fingers. It was a most unusual sensation that I felt. Sharply acute, more driving and penetrating than that which is caused by the male organ, and thrilling to the highest degree. I actually wonder now whether it was more satisfying than a natural fuck. It might have seemed more thrilling at the time because I was dangerously hot. After all, I wasn't over the effects of the strenuous ordeal that I had undergone a few hours before. Now you can readily understand why I found my French maid's touch so electrifying.

As she played with my twat she bent over and breathed into my ear soothingly:

"Ah, Meess Flossie, I'll bet eet feels so nice . . . such a deleecious birdie . . . eet sucks on my finger like eet do on a beeg preek, n'est pas?"

"Oh, Maybelle . . . you are naughty, it's so nice . . . ah . . . so good!"

"Your birdie, she seeng weeth delight . . . my birdie she want to seeng too."

By that remark she must have meant that she wanted me to reciprocate. That is the way I analysed it. Then suddenly the memory of that evening when I told Aunt Stella about my cherry-busting experience came to me. I recalled how we finger-frigged each other till our passions were eased. As a result I said:

"Maybelle, stop! Take off all your clothes . . . I am so selfish to forget that you have a cute nest between your legs . . . it likes the same things mine does too?"

"Mees Flossie, you ees a peach . . . so

thoughtful. I love eet . . . I love to have you do eet to me!" She spoke as she began to undress.

"Do you have any idea when Roland will be back? I wouldn't want him to catch us this way."

"Roland, he ees a nice man, he would say notheeng. See, I am so anxious I sheever!"

"Gee, your skin is so nice and white, just like milk. I'll bet you taste as good as you look! Mmm-mmm, hurry, I am getting hungry for you!"

"And I have always wanted to do theese to you, evair seence I have first seen you . . . I like you a lot, Meess Flossie!"

She had eliminated her last piece of clothing . . . she stood nude. Her body was the double of Blanche's. You will remember how I felt towards her; I desired my French maid's even more strongly. Why? There was an obvious answer. I knew her, she was my confidante and she no doubt looked upon me with extremely good favour. That's reason enough!

"Just a meenute, Mees Flossie, I forget sometheeng," she said, racing from the room.

She reappeared a few seconds later, carrying two rubber hoses . . . they appeared to be from douche bags.

"What in the world have you got there? What are those for?"

"Ah, Mees Flossie, be a leetle beet calm,

I have a new idea, we air going to geeve eet a try. Yes?"

"I'll try anything one time . . . hurry, my cunnie is itching to beat the band!"

"Move ovair, I'm comeening right een! Now do everytheeng like I do."

She took the two pipes and gave me one. They were each about eighteen inches long, well greased, and free from any nozzles.

"Here, you take thees," she offered, as she entered the bed with her face near my slit and mine, vice-versa.

She immediately dug her tongue into my twat. I followed as I was previously directed. Her tongue was keen and very firm. Its heat was terrific, and so was the itch in my pussy. She began to shove the tube into my crack, but no unusual sensations were felt. Everything she did I copied. When she had sunk the tube all the way in so that only about an inch remained on the outside, Maybelle applied her mouth to the free end. She buried it deep enough in her mouth so that she could press her lips to my cunt-loaves. My pussy seemed to take a great liking to this. Her lips were so tepid; I guess mine were too because as I bore down upon her mellow, fleshy twat she gasped and sucked my hole more feverishly.

I could feel the inserted tube touching my belly. Without a warning she blew a puff of hot air into the tube and then drew it slowly out.* Oh, my gosh! What a sensation! What a tremendous shiver my body made! My breath stopped! I was paralysed by a shock of colossal joy. When she blew on it, it seemed as though my uterus was being filled with hot steaming spew and when she withdrew the air . . . oh I can't describe it! I can say this, though: There are times when we haven't jazzed for a real long time and when we do, after a long lay-off we sometimes feel as though we are going to lose our vaginal tubes . . . it just draws that tight when we come. With a man I'm told it is the same way, only in his case his prick is sucked way into his belly and it bobs in and out . . . it seems as though the dick is apt to be swallowed by the stomach, there is such a tremendous inward pressure.

Since I have explained this I will show you the reference that it has to the sensations that I felt when Maybelle blew and withdrew air in and from my uterine cavity. The feeling was of this order, but it was so much more intense and absorbing.

Gee! I wish I could describe it . . . it seems that anything pertaining to the stimulation of the cunt cannot be described . . . it just feels so good! It is the only emotion and the only thing in this universe that cannot be

* Publisher's note: readers are advised not to attempt this curious practice, it may damage the health of the participants.

adequately or picturesquely worded. It is the one thing that makes me feel so utterly helpless and infantile when I try to convey it to the readers' senses. Only those who have gone through the act will fully appreciate and understand how I felt during the many prick-visits to my sensitive womb.

I wanted to scream when my maid blew and sucked on the pipe which was buried deeply in my undulating trap. I couldn't because my mouth was firmly adhered to her box. I couldn't have released it even if I had wanted to . . . some mesmeric force hidden in her two torried cunt-lips seemed to hold me there. This pulsating deliciousness magnetized my mouth to it. It tasted better than maple syrup and honey combined! You must know it was savoury . . . supinely so! And this was only the first time I ever sucked a cunt, so you can well imagine the course I followed in the future.

Instead of screaming when this air blazed my coozie, I puffed . . . and it WAS a puff. She clutched my head between her legs, heaved, rolled and bore her mouth further into my crack. Then I felt another load of her electrifying breath, mightier than the first. I clinched her head with my legs. We were both by this time rolling about, squirming and fighting to free our locked-in-the-cunt heads. I couldn't hold it in any longer, I had to emit a hearty, lustful yell. I would burst if I couldn't. I felt that she wanted to do the same, but was I in a condition where I could release her head? My legs seemed to be forged about her head and my sucking cunnie was trying to draw it in. One more breath of air in the hose, I felt, would have caused me to die a death of joy, if I couldn't shriek from the blissful thrills. I was beginning to come and I just have to moan when I do this . . . everyone does; that's the sign of real enjoyment, I guess.

Even though I wanted to free my head I locked my arms around her ass and blew and lapped more feverishly. I even tried to chew her cunt, she had me so extremely excited. Her cunt-tube was beginning to get tight around my mouth. She grasped the tube in my slit between her teeth and pulled it back and forth. She must have had a very hard time doing this, even though she only moved it an inch in either direction. Can you imagine how that felt? No, don't try, you'll never know—not until you do this. Feeling an eighteen-inch tube that was fitted snugly to my shaft and inwardly to my uterus, drawing the gelatin-like flesh inward and outward—my shaft was actually moving up and out. Let me repeat: every inch of the surface was rubbed by this hot rubber, from my cunt-orifice to the interior of my womb. No prick ever covers a woman that thoroughly.

I could stand it no longer, I burst forth:
"Oh it's so wonderful . . . do it, do it! Oh

ooo-ooo . . . mm-m . . . so heavenly! Mayb-elle, do it . . . keep on doing it! I'm dying! It's so good!"

By the way her cunt was tightening up I calculated that we would both come at the same time; this would never do. I could reason, excited as I was, that if this happened we might not be able to suck every last drop from each other and give that fast workout that is so necessary to complete a successful spend. I slowed down so that I would come first . . . I wasn't taking any chances, either one of us might swoon at the climax and I for one didn't want to be left holding my package.

My cunt soon strode out in front. I mean by that, that it was nearer to the point of coming than hers . . . I could feel it. A bolt, not any less powerful than one of lightning, seemed to strike me. My twat choked the rubber to an immovable tightness. My stomach, heart and every organ from my hair to my soles, began to throb . . . yes, that pulsating feeling spread to every part of my body, like a match thrown on a surface covered with gasoline. I couldn't help myself, my mouth dug its way further and further into her coozie. I wanted to eat it! I wanted to swallow it! I wanted to drown in her juice! I WAS CRAZED! So damned crazed and furious. That bolt increased in intensity . . . it became gigantic, majestic, colossal and so heavenly blissful! Whew! Could I undergo such an orgasm? Wouldn't it leave its permanent marks?

Afraid as I was to approach the climax, I couldn't stop . . . there was a most thrilling, gnawing sensation at my heart. There was a supinely delicious tugging feeling at the pit of my stomach. And the feeling in my cunt tube? Don't ask! It was thrilling beyond description! More enjoyable than being fucked by three pricks at one time—one in the mouth, another in the ass and still another in the twat. Boy, oh boy! That is a feeling, but this was still better! All I can say is get your best girl friend and try it immediately.

In spite of my trying to make myself come first and my confederate second, we both spent at one time. And when we shot we both quivered and squirmed about the bed like two victims with a St. Vitus' dance in every muscle. I think I bit a piece of her cunt out . . . at least mine was rather sore for some time afterwards.

That is all that I can remember, because we both swooned in delight. I awoke to find Maybelle working frantically over my body with a cold towel. My tongue felt like it was almost torn from my mouth. It was very tired and sore. My neck ached, partly from this experience and partly from the one with Carl. Gee, I'll never forget it so long as I live!

"How do you feel, Meess Flossie . . . eet was wonderful! Yes?"

"It was gloriously so . . . we must do it oftener . . . we will?"

"You bet, cher amie. Meess Flossie, I theenk you air wonderful! Just a meenute, somebody reengs."

She hustled from the room to answer the door. I covered myself and pretended to be sleeping. I didn't want Roland to know what I had indulged in. It might not have made any difference, but what a man doesn't know about a woman seldom hurts him. He was the only person who I thought could call at that time. Of course it could have been Carl, but he, I thought was too drunk to return to the apartment. It was Roland—I heard him inquire about me.

A few seconds after Roland entered I heard the bell ring again. I heard him greet his son. I felt that I was in a terrible predicament. Carl might still be drunk, I thought, and tell Roland about the events earlier in the day. I breathed a long sigh of relief when I had determined that he was serenely sober. I heard Roland's footsteps approach my door. I thought that it would be best for me to feign sleep. He opened the door, peeped in and silently departed. I was in neither the proper mood nor condition to see my lover.

That evening I did not leave my bed. I needed rest . . . plenty of it! I slept through that night as though I was under the influence of a drug. Maybelle, I later learned, told Roland that I wasn't feeling well.

The next day while Roland, Carl and I were eating our evening meal at the apartment my lover did not look as though he was free of mind. Something seemed to be troubling him. Immediately I thought he had discovered what I had tried to do to his son. If it was that I was going to let him bring the topic up . . . I'd have been foolish to have done so myself. After chatting for a few minutes about nothing in particular we ran out of conversation. There was a moment or so of silence. Then as though something was going to hurt him terribly, Roland began to speak hesitantly.

"Flossie and Carl, I don't know why I have withheld from saying this so long, but I must make a trip to London next week."

"Business, dad?" asked his son, frowning.

"I wish that it were that . . . no, I wouldn't have held back so long if such was the case. I must undergo an operation, although not a very serious one. Now, Carl, I want you to be nice to Flossie while I'm gone and treat her like you would a sister. It will only be about two or three weeks at the most."

"What kind of an operation is it? It is only right that we should be with you."

"No, it isn't that serious . . . just a minor throat ailment."

"But I still insist that Flossie and I should be at your side."

"I'll tell you what, you two go to Deauville, I will join you both there later."

After dickering with him for a few moments we submitted to his plans. Deauville, if you haven't heard, is a famous, ultramodern watering place in France. Only the most fashionable, the sporting class and the bizarre French models are to be found inhabiting this resort. There they go to display their voluptuous bodies in wanton and obscene costumes.

After we had completed our meal I walked over to Roland and kissed him in daughterly fashion. I thanked him for wanting us to go to this seashore. In glee I whispered:

"You dear, I will give you an extra delicious love feast to remember me by tonight."

❧ 6 ❧

6

That night my maid prepared me most carefully for a night of lustful orgy. She, as you have read, was a skilled coquette and an expert in synthetic aphrodisiacism. She massaged me with strong wine, then with perfumed creams. She also douched my sexual organs with incensed waters and cantharides, then combed the pluffy curls of my pussy until they were like silk. She completed her job by cloaking me with a thin layer of powder.

"Meess Flossie, you air feet for a keeng! I weesh I could do eet weeth you again but I must not make peeg of myself."

Then she drew over my shapely body, which incidentally sparkled with virgin freshness, a thin transparent pair of silk tights. It moulded to my figure as though I had been poured in to it. It reached from my toes to my neck and had three openings, two from which my nipples stood saucily and deliciously out, the other opening between my legs. This was so arranged as to allow only my pussy's pulpy lips to be uncovered.

The entire costume revealed to perfection the fluffy tufts of my silken hairs and moulded my beautiful round you-love-to-feel-it bottom. Not a single one of my many alluring curves and dimples were missed . . . every one was draped to the greatest advantage.

"Ah, Meess Flossie, you can make any man crazy weeth desire een thees . . . eet makes you look . . . how do you say? Sensuous. Thees seelk, eet sure make you look so nice. Roland he weel be threeled more than usual. You know when eet rubs against a man's body eet adds such a threel!"

"I am so lucky to have you as my maid, Maybelle. You have taught me so very much and caused me such happiness."

"I do all thees because I like you, cher amie."

She noticed me most closely as she fixed my hair. I too began to survey myself in the mirror. As I noticed the added lewdness that this outfit gave my body I felt a hot lascivious tremor shake me all over. My cunnie began to itch and swell.

Maybelle, always on the alert for tokens of lust, immediately recognized my feelings as revealed by my flushed face and convulsive twitchings of my body.

"Mees Flossie," she spoke, saucily winking her eyes and shrugging her shoulder, "if I had what you Amair'can ladies call a preek, I would make you feel much better than you do now. I would do eet to you now but tonight ees Roland's."

"You are always so thoughtful and understanding . . . I could never get along without you."

"I have a peecture here, I want you to do eet tonight een thees position . . . eet ees marvelous!"

She showed me a photo of a man and woman jazzing in a position that was entirely new to me. They were lying with their heads in opposite directions, each other's crotch hitched . . . of course the man's cock was in her twat. His feet were at her bubbies, tickling them, apparently in a most delicious and lewd manner.

"Mees Flossie, eet ees one grand way. You weel try eet . . . yes, tonight?"

"Maybelle, you know anything that you tell me to do is good. Of course I will!"

I wore a negligee of black transparent silk that evening as a coverall. It was one of the many recent purchases added to my pink and lacy wardrobe. There were such things as other tights and exquisite lingerie. I draped myself in this robe of diaphanous silk so that I could surprise Roland with these tights. Needless it is to remind one, how alluringly and lovely a contrast was affected by the milky whiteness of my skin sifting through this black silk outfit. I then awaited for the propitious moment to arrive.

Later that evening, when Roland clasped me in his arms, he had no idea how I was dressed underneath. After several fond and loving kisses he remarked that he did not feel like indulging in a cock and cunt embrace that evening. But I had other plans. With a rougish twist of my bottom I said:

"We shall see, dear . . . just a minute."

He had seated himself in a comfortable chair. He, as it was his custom when retiring, wore silk pyjamas.

I walked over to the middle of the room where I wiggled from my gown. There I stood, a vision of provoking voluptousness. I shall never forget the way his eyes suddenly brightened as they found me.

As his stare fixed itself upon me he gloatingly emitted an expression of delight.

"Good heavens!" he said, "what a cockdish you are!"

Instantly he uncovered his tool, which was soft, drooping over his hairy balls. I posed artfully, exposing to the greatest advantage every one of my symmetrical curves. When I had turned my back to him and he saw my impudent bottom he gasped:

"How ravishing!"

As I looked his way I saw him clasp his tool in his hand, and squeeze and jerk it convulsively. His face beame distorted by lust as he gloated over his lecherous joy. His magnificent tool had attained an exceptional size and stiffness.

Show me the man that would not get a beautiful hard-on if he could gaze at the same picture of carnal delight that Roland looked upon! I know any man with a little spew left in his balls could not prevent himself.

I danced over, sat on his lap and twined a loving arm around his neck. I placed the knob of his turgid dick in my hand and squeezed it while I kissed him with all my tongue.

I began to boil in passion. My quim was getting moist and the cantharides were doing their work too. I pressed my bubbies to his face, and the nipples tickled him in the eyes, ears and nose.

"Now, Roland . . . prick, prick, prick me with a prick. Doesn't my big boy feel like doing it to me? Wouldn't you like to see what your big fat thing is able to do?

"Flossie, you little devil, you have made me drunk with your beauty. Come, let's get into bed but don't take off those tights. You are so soft and dreamily exquisite in them . . . come!"

He removed his pyjamas, stretched himself out on the bed and awaited me. This time he appeared more anxious than I. I raised my cunnie box over his face and presented him with a full view of my swollen quim. I knew my lover would adorn the passion quivering lips with one of his soothing French kisses.

It was disappointment this time, because he was excited to impatience. My attire had affected him so strongly and had put him in such an excited and rampant condition that he appeared giddy with passion. Even the dainty aroma which emitted from my pussy had an added amount of lust and deeply inebriated him.

Since first putting on those tights, I had felt extremely maddened. The part that I had just played had a very strong tendency to increase this emotion. I really wanted him to chew my cunt-lips until they bled. I looked again to see his tool standing like a pillar and perhaps that strong too. Its head was inflamed to a ruby red.

"Sit on it, Flossie!"

After kissing and running my tongue in the eye I squatted on it. Very little trouble was experienced by my cunnie in swallowing his monster, despite its unusual size, for my twat was well lubricated with the reeking oils of passion. His splendid affair did stretch me though as it sunk slowly into me. Soon I felt the turgid head beating all the way in, almost to my uterus.

I think this time I was tighter than usual. I felt that way. I blamed it on my maid's treatments. It felt so good when I lowered myself that I had to cry with agonizing, heart-chewing pleasures. I pushed down and almost tore the skin from his tool . . . that's how tight I was!

"My heavens, girlie . . . darn but you're tight! Your pretty little titties never looked more tempting and fuckable! You certainly are charming in that black outfit . . . ah, how lovely it is to feel you screw me!"

Whenever I am screwing and a person talks to me like this, it excites me immensely and spurs me onwards in greater enthusiasm. I guess the same psychology can be applied to this situation as the reaction of a team to the lusty rooting of their college backers.

Prompted by an impulse to give him an added attraction, I raised myself, rested on my feet so that no part of my body touched him—only my tight gripping cunnie held his peter intact. In this position I moved slowly up and down, letting it almost slip out, then with a vigorous dynamic thrust I would again resheath it to its entire length.

"Ye Gods!" was all that he could utter.

It was wonderful . . . I have never as yet seen a man enjoy it as much as he did. Yes, without a doubt Roland enjoyed my quim with the utmost satisfaction. His eyes would roll wildly, then close, in this sensational contact limited only to the sexual parts. It was all too exquisite, too lovely to withstand. It overwhelmed me after I had spent a second time ahead of his load. I deliciously deluged his joyous tool with the simmering oils of my love well.

"Ah, your sweet honey, how wonderful and good it feels when you drop it on my balls . . . screw again that way . . . it's heavenly . . . so . . . so . . . good!" he panted for breath. "What a fucker! Mm . . . oh . . . suck it with your nippers . . . pull it . . . it . . . it . . . it's coming . . . oh . . . oo . . . o . . . o . . . oo . . . o. . .!" He almost yelled as he finished, so great was his ecstasy.

I twisted upon his tool, sucked and pumped it all at the same time. I also occasionally pinched his joint with my strong nippers. I was giving him the ride of his career.

Heavens! Boy, he shot hard! Oh such a creamy delicious spend . . . the warm spew felt so nice trickling through my vaginal tube into my uterus. When I came down his jets shot high into my quim. I could feel the molten shots strike within.

Ye gods! Did I spend when I felt this? I did! And how voluptously I did! I washed his cock and balls very thoroughly with my juice. I screamed and dropped heavily, sheathing his tool in my convulsive pussy. As my orgasm approached it caused my twat to suck on his prick more fervently. It actually sucked the skin from his balls into the hungry lips of my rapacious gash. The splendid stiffness never left his tool.

The moment was ripe to try the new

position that Maybelle had shown and urged me to try. I was too excited and eager to go on to think of anything like calling it a day. No, not me! Never have I left a prick until I have extracted every sign of visible life.

Roland too was in a sexual mood, more lustful than ever if I judged correctly. Anyone in that mind will never balk at any new endeavour of sexual nature ... anything, just so it will make them come!

"Now, Rollie, dear, I want you to lie still and do as I say and I'll show you a new way to do it."

"You sweet lump of fuckable flesh, how can I resist you?"

With his magnificent tool still in me to the hilt, I directed him to turn with me over on his side. We managed to wiggle into the position that I desired, crotch to crotch, rump to rump.

He laughed and cried out in surprise and increased lechery when I placed the bottoms of his feet to my strawberry-ripened nipples. I tickled him under the arms with my toes.

Upon my word, fond readers, I was richly repaid for my new adventure. This new position sent thrills of voluptuous delights through me that I have never experienced otherwise. It is true that we could not very well manipulate our bodies, nor our closely joined instruments of pleasure, but oh how I could squeeze on his deeply immersed tool!

I found that this new posture produced

nerve-racking thrills. They were all enjoyable and delicious, especially when I would
squeeze his prodigiously hard tool! Then
when I would ease my pussy muscles I
would find ravishing ecstasy in the sudden
inflation of the head and its rapid throbbings
. . . oh it was so cunt-tickling! I seemed to
suck it further and further into me. The more
I nipped and squeezed it in the more he
writhed and howled with lustful glee.

It wasn't long before he confessed enjoying
the erotic sensations as much as I.

"Wonderful . . . how good! Flossie, who
taught you that? Gosh, my prick feels like it
is going to explode . . . it's so wonderful!"

"Maybelle taught me . . . isn't it thrilling?
So enjoyable!"

At that moment he was feeling my legs.
He pressed them so lewdly on the ticklish
nerve centres that I could not withhold a
lustful shriek.

When the climax came I was in a blissful
heaven of delight. We both spent together,
our love essences intermingled as we
wallowed in the delirium of our ecstatic
come. His prick reared strongly as he spent
in a futile attempt to free itself from my
muscled, squeezing quim.

Our cries of passion finally subsided to a
low moan. Our legs stretched full length as
we came and then curled up at the toes as
we finished shooting.

In all the diversified positions that I have

been fucked in, none have ever afforded me a climax more ravishing and filled with physical enjoyment.

After the gratification of our passions was completed, we fell into a much needed sleep without even changing positions. His beloved tool, although it became soft, did not shrink. It remained within me until I was awakened by its renewed throbbings. I discovered that it had returned to life and had stiffened within me. The insatiable fires of lust were again rekindled. I was once more prepared for another hot and ravishing feast of coition.

We lost no time in commencing our movements. This time we prolonged the tempestuous climax, that is, checking our inclination to spend. We bathed in this drunken orgy until nature, not to be cheated, demanded her pay. My shrieks were mingled with his groans as every part of our bodies shook and quivered. The muscles of my vagina closed on his distended, rampant cunt-injector, then in a frenzied agony of bliss our overheated sperm mingled in a long, exaggerated, hair curling, pussy-throbbing, copious flood of balsamic, creamy spew. I thought I would never stop shooting.

Totally exhausted and still moaning, we fell into each other's arms and slept far into the next day.

❖ 7 ❖

7

After I arose I prepared myself for my morning bath. As usual Maybelle was at hand to assist me with this task. As she massaged and sponged me, I related the events with my lover of the past evening to her. Her eyes sparkled and her features became crimson from the effect of my tale, for although she was a girl of toil she was a sincere coquette at heart.

"Mon Dieu! I am what you say, hot for a man . . . he must be très grande et très delicieux . . . oo . . . la . . . la!" she exclaimed vehemently, shaking her expressive shoulders then wiggling her saucy, meaty bottom. "I would do anytheeng for such a man. I have one paramour, he ees Amair'can, but he does not know how to do zee baiser Francais (French kiss) and how Maybelle, she do love thees long hot tongue bath een zee birdie . . . oo la la!"

It then occurred to me that I should arrange a party when her lover could be present—that is, after Roland had left and it would be perfectly safe to invite Carl. I, until then, had never attended a fucking party. I wanted to be able to change pricks during a ride. Anyhow I noticed that Carl had often gazed at my maid's ankles libidinously. He didn't seem to remember jazzing her, but I suppose that was because he was too drunk at the time.

She finished making my toilette and then helped me to get dressed. This was the day that Roland was leaving for London and I was intent upon giving him a real nice farewell jazz. This I did with the utmost efficiency.

Carl was on a short business trip and was supposed to return the following day then we would vacation in Deauville.

That same evening Maybelle began to prepare me for bed. I noticed that she seemed to be very nervous and excited. Her eyes were definitely moist. I asked her what her trouble might be.

"Oh," she explained, "my lovair nevair sateesfy me . . . I am so hot between zee legs," she finished, pressing her hands to her excited cunnie.

I felt sorry for her. I for one knew that uncomfortable feeling. I also thought that she was hinting for another lesbian duel. I had the sudden impulse to French kiss her and demonstrate again to her how well I could do it, knowing of course that she so dearly loved the feel of that burning flesh between her legs. A second thought entered my mind. I shouldn't respond to her anxiety because she was only my maid. But after all, no matter what the extent of the differences that hold people of different stations in life apart, or keep different races separated, we stil have one thing in common; we all fuck and like to get fucked.

My eager desire to again lap this French girl's hot twat made the barrier much easier to cross. And I, too, desired the same treatment from this coquette. In a modest but skilful way I proceeded to make my desire known.

"Maybelle, do you remember the last time? Do I know how to French kiss properly?"

"Oh, mademoiselle, would you do eet to your maid again?" she asked, as her features brightened and her eyes sparkled.

"Of course I will . . . it was so lovely! Are you as clean and as attractive between the legs as you were the last time? Let me see it, you have such a pretty little twat!"

I began to raise her dress but she insisted that I stop and we both get undressed. As one piece by one fell, I discovered how attractive she was. After she had removed her maid's costume I discovered that her lingerie was almost as expensive as mine. She wore flimsy-laced, fluffy drawers. Her stockings were of thin black silk and held up by red ribboned garters which were tied in rosette bows. Frankly, I saw a picture of her today that I overlooked the last time I saw her nude. I assume then I was too upset to notice such things. At any rate she was nicer than the mental image that I had formed of her. Yes, surprisingly nicer!

Her thighs tapered from well-shaped hips down to beautiful knees. Her calves were slender and shapely; so were her ankles. A pliant, round, snowy-white bottom jutted alluringly out of the opening in her drawers. After she had removed her corset I beheld a most ravishing pair of dancing bubbies with tips that made beautiful, large, sweet, ripe cherries look sour . . . too good to be left unchewed!

"Oh, Maybelle, what a really beautiful creature you are. I just adore your titties. I would really love to eat them! What nice legs! Let me see your cunnie again!"

She knew exactly what I meant, and I was insane to get my lips on it.

After she had removed all her clothing and stood in graceful abandon, she revealed to me a dazzling picture of French fucksomeness. Below the naval, in a pretty, round, white belly rose a plumpy fullness—a meaty mound, covered evenly and thickly with a black crop of silken, curly hairs. This barely protected the thin, beaming lips of a more alluring slit, which incidentally produced in me some hypnotic desire to devour it. That attractive mound protruded out so plump and fat; it made a pretty crease from the top of her crescent groove to her finely formed navel. How kissable it appeared!

"Goodness, Maybelle," I gloried, "what an adorable pussy! I am in love with it!"

At this time I was seated in a low chair, tasting every feature of hers with my eyes.

She replied in a voice trembling with sexual emotion, moving her lips as though she was inviting caresses: "Mees Flossie, eet ees not nearly so deleescious as yours. I, seence that first time, have always wanted to keess and gamahouche your wondairful birdie!"

"Then let's get into bed where we can kiss each other at the same time."

We both sat on the edge of the bed, then she impulsively threw her arms around my naked body. Putting her right hand between my legs, she pressed my burning slit. She also rubbed my bobbing clitoris as she ran her finger and titillated it most deliciously between the warm, moist, soft, fat lips of my cunnie. There was a vast difference in having a woman do these things to a woman, but it was exciting to me.

Our mouths came together in a lascivious caress, and our tongues also joined in the feast. Hers was long and nimble; she moved it over my lips, lapping most intimately and sensually. She then rolled her tongue around mine, at times endeavouring to swallow mine. By all these movements I assumed that she was showing me how I should use my tongue in her cunnie.

Even while she was busily engaged with her lips and tongue she found enough surplus attention to devote to my slit—it was squirming and steaming hot! In my coozie she dallied her fingers while we bathed each other's love-daggers.

I certainly was aflame! Her diddling finger was about to bring me to a spend. She seemed to sense it; I guess my impassioned moans were tell-tale. She quickly pressed her lips to my bubbies, sucking the nipples and licking the tips with her tongue—the female prick! I screamed as I fully enjoyed the effects of her unusual skill.

"Maybelle, I . . . you make me spend . . . how nice it comes out! And how . . . oh . . . so good!" I gasped and stuttered in my fantastic realms of joy.

When my maid had brought me to this spend, she too was trembling. Her sucking my nipples and playing in my golden gate took its toll upon her too. Her free hand was also employed in tickling my other hard-as-a-rock tit. She had worked herself into such an erotic fury that she could not help but cry:

"Mon Dieu, zee tongue! My birdie . . . she ees wild! Suck eet! Queek suck eet . . . zee tongue!"

I tilted her back on the bed, let her legs

dangle over the side and knelt before her passion-reeked vent. Then I glued my lips to the sweetest cunt that I have ever tasted. I stabbed my tongue into it. I left nothing to be desired . . . everything endearing was ours. I treated this fascinatingly-cunted girl to the most lustful and complete tongue-jazz that I was empowered to bestow. She, beyond any reasonable doubt, enjoyed it. Her bottom heaved and rolled crazily. Many shrieks escaped her lips, and this made me suck more furiously.

It shall always remain a memory hard to forget: how she whimpered and writhed when I reached up and squeezed her titties as she did mine. I, at the same time gave her the fullness of my tongue as I cut every rein that attached me to sobriety. My feminine-prick reached far into her meaty folds . . . how it did thrill her! I know it did! She couldn't even scream. So intense was her ecstasy that she could only lie there, shivering, groaning and gasping. I was then given a most generous volume of French love-dew.

After I had finished her off I was at a pitch where another spend was imperative. I reclined alongside her and renewed my rendezvous with her charms. I became more irritated as I moulded the curly mound below her pretty, snowy-white belly. I spoke to her as she was basking in this delicious mood:

"Maybelle, dear, aren't you going to kiss me? I'm so hot and itchy here," I said, placing her fingers in my slit.

She regained her aplomb: "Oh, Flossie, eet ees so nice and good . . . mmm, deleecious! Would you like zee tongue, oui? I weel geeve eet to you een zee pussy, oui?"

She slipped over me, leaving her bottom and cunt directly over my cunt. She then placed her hand between my wide open, waiting thighs. She pulled the fat lips of my cunnie apart and then gazed lustfully and longingly into my pit. It so happened there was a mirror at the same end of the room that my cunnie faced. In it I could see my gaping slit, the quivering inner lips, and my beating clitoris. Everything in my box was moving and excited.

Directly over my head was Maybelle's coozie, still inflamed and swollen from my sadistic treatment of it—with both my teeth and tongue. Her lily-white bottom with its plump cheeks composed a most striking background for the fluffy fringe around her yawning quim.

My entire interest was directed on Maybelle . . . that is, what she was going to do in the part between my legs. I was getting more restless. I felt like raising it up so that I could imprison her tongue in it—my cunnie's muscles will do a thing like that.

The mirror revealed a striking picture . . . a picture that I shall never forget: one of extreme carnal lust. Her tongue was tickling my clitty and its greedy thrusts into my smolten orifice were most fascinating— maddeningly delightful! The spasmodic opening and closing of her own passionate slit, which was awaiting my tongue and located above my head, seemed to become increasingly excited, as if it was enjoying the same sensations.

She was an expert at this tongue-jazzing art . . . she seemed to know just exactly what kind of a thrust I wanted next. Every time she swabbed my womb I felt a newer and more captivating thrill sweep my quivering form. She tickled my knees and brushed my sensitive belly with the tips of her dangling titties. I was in such an erotic fury that I found it impossible to prolong the cherished agony of a heavenly climax. We were both so frenzied at the point of my spending that we lurched and struggled about like two strangling animals.

She made a twist with her mouth and drew every part of my cunt within; she began to suck like a maniac. I came again—such was the speed of her actions. It was delicious . . . oh so delicious!

I noticed that at the same time I came her slit was opened then it pinched shut and drops of her oozing dew emitted. In my fury I pulled her box down and fully surrounded it with my mouth.

Distorted—oh so very distorted—were our

movements as we sucked each other to another gigantic spend. It was fascinating to watch her white belly quiver and undulate as I jazzed her with my raspy tongue.

For a long time we lay with our legs and arms intertwined, belly against belly, and exchanged obscene thoughts. We discussed the potential hot fuckings that we would like to have.

We talked about Carl. That was a topic I could never overdo. I was in love with the boy—yes, physically and mentally. I wanted my maid's advice in this matter. Maybe she knew ways of enticing men that I did not. At any rate I had nothing to lose by consulting her in the matter—and all to gain.

"You say he do not act like he remember you sucking hees preek?"

"He doesn't act like it."

"That ees queer . . . he weel not fuck me unless he ees drunk . . . Say, Meess Flossie, I just remind myself, he do not seem to remember fucking me. Eef he deed he would try to fuck me when he ees sober, and he do not even say a dirty word in front of me . . . he ees a funny guy, oui?"

"He is very peculiar . . . I don't understand him, do you?"

"Well, no," my maid drawled slowly. "I theenk he may want to keep hees maidenhead for the girl he weel love . . . maybe?"

I wove all the facts of the case together at

this moment and then began to see reality in my maid's suggestion. Could it really be that Carl was a confirmant to that aesthetic doctrine that purity should be the priceless gift to be sacrificed on the altar of matrimony? It seemed incredible that this should be true . . . he was living in a day and age where such fanaticism was no longer the vogue, and his abode was in that part of the world that led the others toward the enjoyment of life through the freedom of sensual passions.

I was inclined to believe in my newly formed conclusion most staunchly. What else was there that would explain the present situation? Evidently he never suspected that his dad was jazzing me—our actions towards one another in Carl's presence were neither conspicuous nor suggestive. And it seemed as though his dad made it a point to jazz me either when his son was out or asleep. Therefore, his attitude and ideas about our relationship could have been none other than his innocent outlook. As you know it is common for one to think of another as he thinks of himself. Perhaps this principle was used by Carl to form the basis of his ideas about our relationship. All these thoughts flashed through my mind as I lay in bed listening to Maybelle's version of the matter.

"But, Maybelle, what shall I do? You know how bad I really want him and I don't think it would be much fun to do it to him while he is drunk."

"Well eef that ees zee way you feel about heem then you must be content weeth what you can get from heem . . . you can only get eet away from hees dronk body."

"When he fucked you while he was drunk was it as good as when he is sober?"

"Eet nevair feel good when you do eet to a dronkair, no, no, nevair! But eet feel good when he do eet to me even eef he was not understand what he was doeeng. I can eemageene how wondairful eet would be eef he was sobair. I theenk that I would be sateesfied to fock heem only, eef I married heem."

'Gee, Maybelle, you have me excited . . . gee, I wish I could jazz him this very minute! You surely have made me hot for him!"

"I am sorry, m'dam, but I cannot help eet. I too am hot for heem but I like you so well I would sacreefice my desire for heem een favour of yours. I weel do all I can to help you weeth heem . . . eet must be carefully thought about."

"Maybelle, you are so nice to me . . . gee, you're so different than most women; they would all fight with each other for the chance and here you are actually going to help me!"

We discussed every possible plan by which we might trap Carl and steal his maidenhead . . . it really wasn't a maidenhead because he must have fucked every time he became

194

drunk, but still, he never experienced the sensations because he never seemed to have any recollection of them. In other words, getting fucked was (till then) an unexperienced sensation so far as Carl's prick was concerned.

We thought of getting him into a room and locking the doors and then stripping. We would then do everything that was humanly possible to make him lust-maddened, then to relieve himself of that horrible "nut-ache" he would do the thing we wanted him to do. There was a potentiality that he might jerk off . . . then what?

Then we thought that if we could get someone else to vamp him and take his cherry it might work. Then there was the fact that this must have occurred to him in the past few years because one who has been in the places and with the people that Carl had in the past few years must have met situations similar to the one we planned and he never yielded, so why should he submit to our plan?

My chief objection to trapping him into intercourse was the fact that I liked him and did not wish to do anything that would instil in him an unfriendly attitude towards me. He respected me as highly as he could—that fact was enough to make me forget the first scheme we worked out.

"Maybelle," I said at length, "it's no use,

I can't see any way out. I guess we'll have to let time tell its story."

"Meess Flossie, I do not understand. You must have someteeng een your mind that you do not weesh to deescuss!"

"Yes, you don't mind?"

"Of course not . . . eet ees too personal?"

"No, it is a crazy notion."

"Mees Flossie, I don't want you to forget that these time when Roland ees away ees your best opportunity to do thees. I know that you have fear for heem."

"No it isn't fear. I know he wouldn't say anything if he knew I did it to someone else but I know it would hurt him . . . I know it would!"

"Maybe you air right."

"But still as you say this is a golden opportunity . . . while he is away."

"Maybe when we get to Deauville we may theenk of someteeng, oui?"

We then disgressed from this topic into others pertaining to sexual incidents. Before we were weary enough to retire for that night we both found ourselves in such an excited state from the different fuckings that we talked about that we found it necessary to again indulge in another soothing twatembrace.

Maybelle remembered an old position that she had once tried with a friend of hers.

It was a position very similar to the one Roland and I tried with rump to rump and crotch to crotch. The difference in this: *both* of us split our legs and opened our cunts.

The picture that reflected in the mirror was exciting—exciting indeed!

"Thees ees what you call le baiser de l'con . . . een Anglaise eet means the keess of zee conts."

"Oh, it's go good . . . push harder . . . ah . . . nice!"

"Ooo la la, mon cher amie . . . eet ees wondairful! Your birdie, she feel so nice zee way eet teeckles mine!"

We tickled each other's titties with our feet. And I don't want to forget to mention how different it is to one's passion to have the tits tickled and to tickle tits with the bottom of the foot and toes. Oh, any part of the body that contacts that soft, fluffy roll of velvety bubbie-meat feels so nice and soothing.

Our mons venerae and our bellies as well as all the hair in these sections was very closely interwoven. Gee, we pressed each other so tight at the crotch that the lining of our tubes seemed to come out and intermingle. Heavens! It was divine! You should have seen how madly we worked our hips and pussies to get our clitties further into one another. The more we rubbed and crushed our slits into one another the greater our frenzy was.

Impulsively Maybelle made a suggestion to this effect: I should rest on my head and shoulders with my feet up in the air. She would stand on her feet, and crush and grind her cunt to mine in opposition. Ye gods! What a position that was! And she knew the art of screwing her cunt around!

She gasped and squirmed as she bore down and twisted with greater zeal. Our cunts felt like they were one, experiencing one feeling, one blissful lust.

I had only to look into the mirror to see another picture that could rightfully be filed among those titled "The Acme of Sensuality."

We screamed together as we both approached the moment of spending. When our pleasures reached their peak and we finally came we both slumped to the bed in a semi-swoon, our juicy, quivering cunts still glued, enjoying rapturous convulsions of satiation.

When I recovered I exclaimed:

"Maybelle, you certainly gave me a good fuck . . . you are a peach! Gee, I'd fuck you so much if you had a prick . . . you bring that one-come lover here some night and I'll make him so randy he'll jazz both of us all night."

My maid left my chambers for her room and retired. I fell to sleep immediately and enjoyed a most undisturbed night.

8

8

The following day I was most startled because Carl suggested that I must buy a special wardrobe of spicy outfits to take along to Deauville. He mentioned that I should not expect any modesty there but had to sacrifice my feelings to the mood which dominated there—sensuality.

Was there any suggestion in his advice that could make one think other than that he meant fucking is in generous demand and that I too must submit? And wouldn't it seem as though he expected to participate? I was doubtful, though. I did not quite translate his unsaid words into these meanings, yet I entertained a most poignant yearning to do so. I was beginning to know my Carl too well to yield to my yearning.

Carl, thinking that I would err in the choice of my costumes, shopped with me. I bought two bathings suits at his suggestion that would have made a Fifth Avenue lady turn a rich crimson. One was tight fitting, exposing about three quarters of my ass-lumps. This was black, reaching down far enough to cover most of my pussy hairs. It laced at the sides of my hips with yellow ribbons, and you can visualize how little of my fucking machinery was actually covered. At any rate, it would never have want for air. With this outrageously immodest suit came a pair of startling red stockings. They reached just above my knees where they were held in place with rosettes of yellow. From there on my thighs were left bare.

It seems as though the French women adhere to the policy: a little bare flesh well displayed is oftentimes far more tempting than nudity.

This suit was so thin that it freely permitted the pink of my skin to sift through alluringly—extraordinarily!

I also made a most mentionable purchase of dazzling stockings. Some of them were white with fabulously coloured snakes winding around the ankles, some were black with various coloured butterflies interwoven, and still others were short, of unique colours and odd designs.

I couldn't resist trying on the outfits. As soon as I arrived at the apartment. I sported my newly acquired suits. The second suit I bought consisted of a skirt with a fluffy blouse, no sleeves and only a narrow ribbon to hold it around my neck. This left my arms and my entire back, almost to the beginning of my ass-ovals, clearly and defyingly exposed. The skirt was of a sheer flannel, striped in white and black. It reached down to a point midway between my knees and hips. It was full and loose, leaving the limbs exposed and free for action. No stockings were worn with this radical suit . . . it was radical for the Park Avenuers but not for the Deauvillites. Only a woman with lilywhite legs and a creamy, well-formed torso could look nice in this bizarre outfit. With my shapely legs and back I know I must have looked the perfect cock-dish in it!

The cutest and most novel part of this suit was the trunks which were worn beneath the skirt to weakly conceal the rump and pussy. It was split in the centre but laced shut so that it could be quickly and conveniently opened if the occasion required it. Many at the shore must have worn costumes similar to this because all one had to do was to scan the water and see many couples who, no doubt, were jazzing. Their actions were covered, naturally, by neck-deep water.

Oh these French women! How well they know how to excite the passions through suggestive costumes, costumes that make the body more desirable than the nude itself.

When I tried this costume on and paraded before Carl with it for his approval he told me that French women rarely if ever enter the water. Instead they either stroll or lounge on the beach, wantonly displaying their charms. I was truly disappointed because I wanted to swim, a sport that I always will enjoy. He bought me a one piece swimsuit to appease my needs. This suit showed my every contour to its greatest advantage.

I was truly getting impatient for a night of pleasure with Carl. Exposing myself before him, as I did, had its cunt-itching effects upon me, but it did not seem to sway my handsome, desirable prick-endowed Carl. If it did he surely did not reveal it.

"Oh me," I mourned to myself, "pricks are plentiful but what I wouldn't do for one nice prick like Carl's." I had seen it and tasted it; I knew how unimpeachable and egregiously exquisite it really was, not to overlook the tremendous effusion of cunt-wash it was capable of releasing. And to top the situation, it was the biggest prick that I had ever seen—even Maybelle, a girl who had seen an unmentionable number of them, had agreed on this point.

Carl had demonstrated his broadmindness by suggesting the costumes for the beach . . . or did he do this because he understood my desire to be in harmony with the contemporary styles there?·

Carl was becoming a more complex problem as the time flew. He wasn't queer. Apparently he approved of immodest style. His dick had a desire for the feminine meat. His attitude towards women was nonchalant. He rarely, if ever, went out with them. When his conscious mind slumbered—that is, while he was intoxicated—and his subconscious will dominated, he had shown his instinctive need for the feminine flesh.

These are the facts that I had at hand to work with. If I was to enjoy his delectable meat-stick within the next two weeks I must mould all these facts into a chain and find its weakest link. I sat down to figure them out as soon as I finished trying on my new suits.

The only thing that I could think of that might penetrate his philosophical defence against screwing was to re-educate his attitude. Start at the beginning of the laws pertaining to the sins of unchasteness and show why they cannot be considered authoritative and finish this re-education programme by taking him to a public fucking house where they have as part of the vaudeville act different types of screwing, and on the screen (also run as part of the bill), fucking "talkies." In other words the only way I could approach Carl successfully would be through the channels of intellect—first a philosophical discussion of the matter, then life scenes and lastly the actual contact of my craving flesh with his. Men take women's hymens this way—why couldn't I do the reverse to him?

That afternoon, just before our evening meal

I caught Carl in a reflective mood. He was seated in a chair in the library reading a shipbuilding journal.

He was dressed in his smoking jacket . . . he appeared fresh from a bath as his skin was pink and clean. His jacket tended to make him appear more handsome than usual—it was a beautiful orchid with black satin collar flaps. He steadied an antique-looking, straight stemmed pipe in his mouth. The room was filled with the sweet aroma of mellowed, burning tobacco . . . such an intoxicating odour.

At the foot of his comfortable chair there were many pillows. I stealthily walked over and reclined innocently and coyly upon the pillows. He looked up from his magazine:

"Cleopatra," he remarked, trying to sum up my appearance in one word.

"What are you reading, Carl?"

"Just a trade journal."

"Do you mind talking?"

"About what?"

"This and that," I said, turning over on my side and throwing him an innocent, careless smile.

"You're quite definite. I guess you're lonely. Does that size it up?"

"So you do know a few things about a girl's moods . . . where did you learn them?"

"Does it matter?"

"It should . . . after all I think I'm your

sister . . . if . . . if you want to accept me as that."

"Why be so wistful about it? I take it like a course of business."

"Why be so mechanical about it? After all, isn't there anything sentimental or perhaps artistic about it?"

"I seldom look at things that way. I don't know and again I think I do. I guess some things that I call sacred and beautiful, others would perhaps ridicule me for doing so."

"Why, here I have been living under the same roof with you for . . . oh, several months and you haven't even been curious enough to know from where I came and how it happened that I am here . . . doesn't it make any difference to you, Carl?"

"I guess it does. Funny person I am—everything dad does I figure is always for the best . . . I never ask nor criticize. I really should be more interested in who you are and so forth. It's as you said, I guess—you are my sister."

"Don't you think we should be really more intimate with each other, sort of confide in each other as real sisters and brothers?"

"You know it might be, I act this way because I have never had any close relatives. I just don't know how to act towards them."

"We have that in common," I lied so that we would have another mutual element to bind us closer together. "I have always yearned for a brother . . . I don't know . . .

I've sort of had a vision all my life of having a big tall handsome brother like you."

"Aw cut out the mushy stuff . . . I—"

"Now, Carl," I cut in, "I think you've made a confession . . . you think that I'm the same as any one of these Parisian dolls. When I made that remark I meant it, from the roots of my heart . . . you wouldn't command that feeling if you were like other men! You are the perfect realization of my dreams."

"I still think that you are trying to flatter and blind me."

"You think so because you do not understand me as well as I do you . . . I've studied you while you have barely noticed me."

"A woman always does that . . . and, frankly, Floss, I think you are nice. I don't think that I would feel ashamed of you as a sister." He looked into my eyes, trying to reach the back of my skull with his fathomless pools of light.

"Is that a temporary . . . I mean an impulsive conclusion?"

"No-o," he drawled in uncertainty.

"Now, Carl, you know it is." I looked up at him wistfully as I turned over on my side. "If it wasn't you would have paid closer attention to me and we . . . well we really should become more intimate with each other."

"I think we ought . . . even if it's only to

see what that kind of a friendship feels like. I never have gotten that way with a girl yet."

"What makes you shun them?"

"It's like I told you once, they bore me. I guess I have . . . well, sort of a precluded idea about all of them and perhaps I haven't really given any one of them a just trial."

"Gee, Carl, you talk about women as if they were machines—there is nothing mechanical about them. Each one is different . . . everyone has a beautiful and picturesque mind, thoughts so tender . . . softer and dreamier than any artist could paint. Most women live within themselves . . . only men can make them shed their beautiful souls. Your education has made you form a certain idea about everything—call it a mechanical-complex; everything you look at you see as a machine. . . ."

"The human body is a machine, isn't it? It operates like one," he cut in.

"Carl, the body operates like one, yes . . . a perfect machine, but does a machine have brains? Do two like-model machines have individual differences? Is a machine moody?"

"No, I'm afraid it's not any of those."

"A machine cannot serve for more than a few purposes . . . take a woman, a man can forego every machine, every comfort, but he cannot do without woman. She is his sole comforter, she is his palace of amusement, she is his worshipper ... his wife, his mother, she is the missing link of his life!"

"Not in mine," he protested with a smile—there was ice in his tone.

"Carl, I want you to be truthful with me ... have you ever felt that your life was empty, something lacking? It's sort of an empty, sluggish feeling around the heart."

"Yes."

"What do you do when that feeling overcomes you?"

"I want to get away from everything—everything is so boring then. I want a complete change ... I usually get drunk."

"Well, does that seem to help?"

"Yes ... I don't even know I exist then. I'm taken completely away from reality ..."

"Only cowards run away from reality ... an inferiority complex makes one live in dreams—a feeling of inferiority is equal to cowardice."

"Floss, what are you trying to do, make me feel ashamed of myself or what?"

"No, it's not that. I just want to make you understand yourself better. Do you know why you go to drink when you get in that mood? I guess you call it the 'blues' ".

"I told you ... let's hear your slant."

"When a man feels that way—that is when something seems lacking in his life—when he feels as though he is incomplete, only the feminine touch, the presence of an understanding woman, can fill the empty feeling in the heart."

"What you say sounds reasonable—but then, why is it that I get the same comfort out of drinks?"

"You don't, Carl . . . drink is an unhealthy way of changing your moods, which is all that happens."

Was it at this part of the conversation that I wanted to tell him of the action of his subconscious mind while he was drunk. . . ? I did not want to confess to him the incidents of that day. Even in his stupour his soul cried for a woman. He wasn't aware of this.

"What must I do?"

"You know, do I have to repeat?" Then I eyed him . . . he looked like a bashful boy. I spoke, looking at him with a wistful mother-like expression: "Carl . . . I think that what I am going to say is right . . . you are afraid of women. Was it caused by an unsuccessful affair?"

He lowered his eyes, ashamed to meet mine. "No, not exactly."

"Come now, Carl, after all, I'm you're sister . . . you don't have to be afraid."

"All right, here's my story: first of all I want to tell you my attitude . . . that is, the idea I grew up with, what a woman should be. I visualized a woman as being the purest, cleanest creature alive. I dreamed that she should be virtuous, her mind unspoiled by filthy ideas."

"Before you go any further," I broke in, "let me say a few words. Do you realize how humanly impossible it is for a woman to be that way—she must not read, she must not look and she must not hear . . . deaf, mute and blind!"

"You are right . . . but here's what I wanted to tell you: when I was but seventeen I fell in love with a girl my age—I really loved her. I was a virgin, which I still am, and so was she, yet she pleaded with me to . . . you'll pardon me for saying this . . . she wanted me to have intercourse with her. It sickened me to think that a girl so beautiful, so innocent-looking, so nice, with every good and pleasing quality, should want to do a thing like that with me. I figured if she wanted to do a thing like that with a fellow that isn't married to her, then she would do it with most every fellow that she liked before and after marriage. A thing like that would be sort of a gesture of friendship with her instead of one of love."

"I see . . . and, Carl, I think that you are pefectly right." I spoke with a sympathetic tone. The greatest weapons a woman has to use in conquering a man's love are to sympathize with him (he likes to be mothered) and to praise him (he likes to be worshipped).

"That was only my first experience along this line. I have had enough since to make me forget them even as a pastime, yet, I still have hopes of finding one who realizes that one's virginity should be sacrificed upon the altar of marriage instead of to the pagan love god, Eros."

"Carl, I admire you for your unbending and honourable attitude . . . I truly do. It's an amazing coincidence!"

"I don't get you."

After giving him a little sympathy I thought a little praise wouldn't hurt. Like a tonic, you have to mix these two ingredients together in the proper proportions to get the best results.

It was evident that I didn't agree with him nor the answers I gave, but a woman will tell any kind of a lie to get herself the man she desires. If he wanted a woman that way it was up to Flossie to make herself into that woman, yet I don't think there was a man in the world who could make me stop fucking. I just had to be more careful in this case.

"Carl . . . take for example my listening to your tale, if I were as pure in mind as you wanted a woman to be I wouldn't know what you were talking about. Part of one's essential education is sex, so you see how ridiculous your outlook is?"

"You know, Flossie," he drawled thoughtfully, "a dream that one has nursed for so long is pretty hard to give up . . . I guess if I wouldn't do it though I'd be turning my mind back a few hundred years. Your argument is strong . . . I never thought a woman possessed all that reason."

"Carl, it's not my argument . . . it's the world of today . . . after all, we're living in it and we have to make the most of it."

"It's a funny thing . . . in every other problem I've ever faced I have tried to make myself flexible—adapt myself to circumstances—and in this one I forget that ruling . . . funny, very funny," he finished with a satirical grin.

"Now don't you think that we understand each other so much better?"

"Yes and I'm beginning to look forward to many very good times together. I think I can almost see the reason for dad's adopting you. Good old dad, he must have guessed that I needed a sister like you." He looked down at me and his eyes actually sparkled with anticipated happiness.

I too was beginning to feel happy—his resistance to feminine companionship was beginning to weaken. And if I were to be even a poor judge of human nature, I think that the seeds of desire for me were being planted in his heart that very moment.

We heard Maybelle's voice calling us for our evening meal. Carl and I were so absorbed in conversation that we did not seem to pay much attention to the fine dishes that we ate. I began to realize how deeply in love with him I really was. I not only

wanted his prick but him as a whole—
everything about him!

This conversation seemed to open a new
channel for the outlet of his morbid moods
. . . instead of seeking his drinks he sought
me to relieve him of that moroseness.

The following two days found us often
engaged in conversation. I was slowly
breaking his inferiority complex, and after
succeeding with that task I intended to alter
his philosophical outlook. At the most, I had
three weeks to do this in. I had to succeed!
I was becoming more prick-starved as the
time passed—yes, for Carl's.

❧ 9 ❧

9

Two days after our first conversation we left for Deauville: Carl, Maybelle and I. There we registered as sister, brother and maid.

We lost little time until we visited the beach. Frankly, I was shocked: Carl acted like it was medicine that he knew he had to take. Ladies of high social positions, coquettes, actresses and grisettes all in startling creations, lasciviously designed outfits, purposely made to tempt and fascinate men, were promenading about and littering the beach. Never before had I ever seen so many seemly-shaped, good-looking women congregated at a public beach. Even King Neptune and his horde of enticing mermaids could not equal this sight. I was stunned by the sight of so many pretty legs, arms, shoulders and the make-you-want-to-fuck-them bubbies. The average suit there left these two irresistible mounds of meat half-nude.

Most of those who wore one piece suits were actresses . . . they must have shaved their cunt-hairs, because if they hadn't they surely would have peeped out. The strip that covered their crotches was only about two to three inches wide—barely enough to cover their cunt-mouths. The average French actress is a different type of beauty than the American . . . they are almost exclusively the wanton type. In spite of this field of strong competition I felt that I could hold my own.

I knew what Carl admired in a woman and it certainly wasn't what the average visitor at Deauville possessed. If I were to act like one, it would arouse Carl's disgust and if I didn't I would feel completely out of place. Realizing the problem I faced, I went to Carl and explained it to him. He, I guess, out of pity agreed that I would have to act like the mob and also promised that it would not arouse his distaste. This made me very happy for more than one reason. If I expected to get jazzed regularly I had to be able to tempt at least one prick a day.

I was beginning to feel the need for an excessive, lustful orgy. I hadn't been stabbed by a prick since four days before and by tongue, three days. I was in a very trying situation; I hoped Carl would not stick too close to me.

The sights that greeted my eyes at this resort also tended to raise my desire for lust. The wanton displays, the lascivious vibration of the hips—every action seemed to instill one with the mood—the mood that the crowd in general adopted. I could not understand how Carl could mingle with this lust-enthused group without being overcome by their contagious fever. It just seemed to creep into one's blood! To jazz, to jazz! Men were openly feeling the women's charms; big pricks could be seen blanketed by bathing suits, hardly any were protected by athletic supporters. My cunnie was itching for one of those big pricks. Even a substitute would do for my enraged slit.

Carl and I swam about until I tired. I proposed that we should get dressed but he insisted that I should wait on the beach until he swam out to one of the yachts and back. I consented because it was an opportunity that I was looking forward to all day. It was my only chance of getting a bit of cunnie lotion without being detected by him.

I adjusted my bathing suit in my dressing room and tinted my face with a coating of cosmetics. The bath houses were most unusual. They were private, built on wheels, and each was equipped with a cot, mirror and dressing table. I, at first, actually wondered what purpose the cot served. After I prepared myself I returned to the beach. Carl, I noticed, was far out, en route to the craft that he wished to overtake.

If you will remember I had my one piece suit on. My entire back was completely bared—so were my bubs, almost to the nipple points. The two full cheeks of my bottom were tactfully exposed by the artfully designed cutout of the legs.

It seems as though people had overlooked me when I strutted the beach with Carl . . . it must have been so. When I swished across the beach this time to our umbrella I heard many sighs and "ohs" and so forth from the women, and gasps of desire from the men. Perhaps it was while I walked with Carl none of the women noticed me but they fancied Carl while the men seeing that I was accompanied did not pay heed.

After I had made my way to our spot a tall handsome Frenchman approached me. He introduced himself as Count du Crannes. He appeared to be well bred and perfectly mannered. His desire to be courteous was excessive; so was his flattery. Indeed he was a charming man, the type that fascinate a woman quickly and deeply. My intuition told me that he was both a gentleman and a connoisseur of feminine pulchritude.

I did not blame him for summoning enough courage to introduce himself. I had unflinchingly and boldly strutted from the bath house exhibiting my charms with reckless abandon. My blonde curls and neatly carved, almost entirely denuded form were enough to make any man notice me and become strongly hungry for my flesh. When I walked down the steps cocks stood up . . . a tribute to me.

As he chatted to me about the elegance of

our surroundings and the intoxicating charms that I owned I saw his peter very definitely hardening in his abbreviated attire. At the rate that he was becoming overwhelmed by his passions it didn't take long until he was drunk enough from the influence of my gifted body to ask me whether or not I would let him use it for a while.

"Mademoiselle," he marvelled, "eet ees a great honour zat you do me . . . just for you to let me speak to you make me vair' happy. Ah but you zee mondaine of zees resort. I do not know eef you have come here for zee . . . ah . . . er . . . diversion or zee batheeng?"

"Francois, I have come here to enjoy myself," I encouraged.

"I would like to asseest you een doeeng so. Eet would be my greatest plaiseer. I have noteeced you weeth handsome man. Ees he your escort?"

"No, just a brother."

"Then you come here weethout a lover?"

"Yes. Do you know where I can find one?" I looked at him and laughed sarcastically, perhaps because he seemed so sensitive. I knew he wanted to jazz me but he seemed a mite uncertain of his power. Look how much time could be saved if men could only read the prick-seeking mind.

"May I suggest . . . you do not theenk I am a conceit eef I suggest Francois du

223

Crannes," he smiled with a lot of confidence. "He ees worth zee chance."

"Why do you think so?" Make them work for their tail, they like it better.

"Well, mademoiselle," he burst enthusiastically. "I am appreciative of your peteet charms. I am een love weeth you!"

"Now, Francois, you know it is impossible to fall in love in such a short time."

"Weeth you ... Meess ... er .. .."

"Miss Flossie," I put in.

"Meess Flossie, notheeng ees eemposeeble weeth you. I love you zee first meenute I see you ... you air so charmeeng ... so beautiful!"

"I am sorry," I teased.

"But, Meess Flossie, I need you ... you cannot do zeese to me ... please!"

"But I can!" I wanted to see how much I could make him plead before he would leave.

"Meess Flossie, eet has been my experience zat eef a lady, she dress and act so to tempt men she must have raison for doeeng so ... you come here weethout lovair ... evairy woman need a lovair."

"I think you are right ... but every woman chooses her lover."

"That ees her preevelege."

"Ill be frank with you, Francois," I spoke with brutal coldness, "you are nice looking, you seem to be well bred and a gentleman ... but how do I know that you shall make an excellent lover?"

"I must be given an opportunity to prove eet!" He spoke with renewed courage.

"This is not the place," I said glancing at him pertly.

"Meess Flossie, what ees the number of your bath house? I weel meet you there een five meenutes, oui?"

"Number ten. Do you really want to?"

"Weeth all my soul!"

Saying no more, I hurried to my bath house. As I ascended the steps I looked out into the water to see how much time I would have before Carl would return. He was about fifty metres from the yacht; I calculated that I had more than half an hour and if he rested aboard before he returned I would have more time.

Of course this rather bold-faced act had to be accomplished with utmost precaution. I looked about and stole into my hut while no one was looking. I left the door unlocked. About five minutes later François entered and locked it.

I pretended to be terribly shocked when he tried to crush me in his arms ... I repulsed him. He was getting so excited and rampant ... he made a pitiful sight. I could scarcely find the will to prolong his agony. I too was becoming randy. The swelling in his bathing trunks was growing and throbbing most tumultuously. Suddenly he made a mad lunge for me with his arms. He caught me and crushed his rigid organ to my passionate one. My cunnie was itching and burning for a big monster . . . like the one that was caressing the part in my legs.

It was most painful for me to conceal my feelings but when he fought to remove my suit I could resist him no longer.

"Wait, I'll undress for you . . . you are a captivating lover?"

"I am een love weeth you, n'est-pas?"

Immediately he pulled off his bathing suit and—heavens! What an enormous tool he had! Just the type I was yearning for. Need I say more? You can well imagine its reaction upon me. I lay down on the couch. His eyes blazed as they explored every crevice of my lasciviously posed body. He dropped to his knees and kissed me all over, burying his face in my crack and jazzing it with his lips and tongue like mad. I wanted something more blissful and satisfying than this. I was hot . . . oh, so hot from not being jazzed for four days.

"Francois," I cried, "put your big thing in me—hurry!"

He responded instantly. He was atop me and soon I felt the turgid, throbbing knob of his pulsating giant plow its way towards my uterus. Gosh, it did hurt, but how I loved that agonizing hurt! The pleasurable pain of a big prick plowing and ripping its way far into my belly. Before he had it fully inserted into me I shivered under the spell of an ecstatic quake—my first come in four days.

I wound my fat legs around him and squeezed his body closer to my cunt. I wanted every bit of his form that my cunt was capable of swallowing. The spasm of pleasure deluged me. I was no longer sane, just a squirming shaking fuck-o-maniac!

I coaxed him into a frenzy of lustful action—oh my, how lovely and fast he screwed me. Before I knew it I was again shrieking from the bliss and convulsions of another dew-emission. Then he came!

He groaned and mumbled as he worked his bottom up and down.

"Oh, Mees Floss! Mon peteet Floss . . . eet ees wondairful . . . raveeshmen . . . ooo . . . ooo . . . oh . . . Mon Dieu! My preek eet ees so good!"

As he cried I felt hot gushers of his spew oiling my jazzing machinery. It squirted in long piercing jets against my womb, like needles. I swooned and saw many star-like objects in my semi-consciousness. We jazzed another round and I would have gone more, but I was afraid to do so in spite of the fact that the second round still left him with a hard-on. Carl would soon be back.

Half-satisfied he arose and donned his suit. I told him where to meet me that night at an hour long after Carl's retirement time. Then, I promised him, we would finish what he had so wholeheartedly begun to enjoy.

"Carl, when does dad say he is arriving?" I

asked one day during the middle of our second week at the resort.

"He says between now and a week from today."

"Won't it be nice for us three to get back together again? I'm beginning to feel so lonesome for him."

I really wanted to find out how much longer I had before he would return. If I had one more week I figured I might be able to jazz Carl. What raised my courage so high was, the day before, while we were romping about the sands in a joyous mood I told him about a wonderful show that they were going to have next week. I told him it was a rumour that I had heard . . . my maid actually told me about it. In reality, it was going to be a legitimate vaudeville act first, then a jazzing act, followed by a jazzing picture. Of course Carl didn't have to know this and I would act like I didn't. Once we were inside, I planned that I would consent to staying. "Just to see how indecent and immoral this world was getting to be." Those were the words that I intended to use.

We digressed from the topic of his dad's return into other topics of conversation until, exhausted by talking, we ultimately decided to go in swimming.

This day I wore my blouse and skirt suit, the one with a split in the drawers for my coozie to breathe from. My coozie really needed to breathe a prick in that day.

Carl entered the water first and complained that it was a bit chilly, just the temperature he liked. I entered. The water was too cold for my comfort so we separated, I to the beach and he to the deep waters. He had a friend at anchor there and I noticed that he began to swim in that direction. This meant that he would be gone for at least an hour . . . an hour which I desired to spend with a pleasure-giving prick.

I sauntered about the beach for a few moments then reclined beneath our umbrella. I suppose as usual, every man noticed my freely shaking hips and my well-displayed, saucy, dimpled knees. I lay for a few moments wondering which of the pebbles I had attracted mostly and which would roll up to me for that much desired jazz. To my dismay and disappointment an elderly American gentleman of evident refinement accosted me, introducing himself as Senator Adams. His unusual flattery made my head swim. I was not used to receiving such compliments from a man his age. He must have been sincere because I was almost certain that he was beyond the age of fertility. I could reason no profitable selfish motives on his part.

"Surely," I said to myself, "this man is over fifty and could not very well have need for a fresh young girl like myself, a girl who demands the vitality of a man much younger.What could he mean by making such ardent advances to me?" I was growing very curious. I thrived upon adventures so why should I shun this possible one? I didn't. I guess like the average woman I wanted to see the outcome of it.

After talking a while he boldly said:

"My dear young girl, won't you have compassion for an old man who cannot enjoy female charms like a younger man?"

"What do you mean, Senator?" I asked, deeply puzzled.

"Take me to your dressing room and I will show you . . . ah, you little Venus," he continued ranting," I would like to fondle your delicious body all over and feel your pretty legs. I will give any sum of money that you might ask to enjoy that privilege."

As I was rich in wealth I spurned the wage. It was so reminiscent of prostitution.

"No, Senator, you mistake me. Money—that kind of money—is of little value to me. I dare say that I am wealthier than you. You do interest me though and if you are very careful, if you don't frighten me, I will let you come to my room. You won't ask for too much?"

This promise brought many counter-promises from him. He promised me anything from special privileges to a seat in Congress if I returned to the good old U.S.A.

I told him where to meet me. Five minutes later he entered. He was dressed in a white flannel yachting suit, a red necktie—a very soft hue of red—and a white pair of shoes. His grey hair and distinguished looking face made an impression upon me as he entered. It reflected true aristocracy. I actually felt timid before him. He didn't seem the type to indulge in what was soon to follow.

It soon developed that he had indulged too freely and carelessly during his life and had passed the age when a man can have a normal erection.

"Well," I asked, "what is it that you desire of me?" careful not to be offensive.

"Oh, my dear," he spoke in a husky voice, "how I wish I were a young man again and I could enjoy you in the good old fashioned way. Please undress and I will show you how I get my pleasure?"

"But how will I get mine?"

"Rest assured my dear, you will get yours too."

There was nothing left to do but get undressed and await developments. I stripped in a jiffy. I insisted the Senator do likewise, not because I wanted to see him nude but because I didn't want him to dirty his immaculate clothes.

He became more nervous and excited as he undressed. When he had completed with his disrobing he walked over to me. His knees quivered with emotion. He passed a hand caressingly up and down my leg and over my milky, plump bottom; then my bubbies became the objects of his ensuing attention. He immersed his face into my pussy, kissed its soft, thick, pliant lips and whimpered:

"What savoriness! What tastiness! You are truly a lover's dish! Ummmm." And he buried his face again into my quim.

I noticed a sad spectacle between his legs. There hung a midget peter and a pair of shrunken balls. Impulsively I took them in my mouth and rolled my tongue around them.

"That feels so good . . . pet . . . dearie! Jerk it, darling," he muttered.

I squeezed the root between my thumb and finger, and held the head firmly between my lips and with the other hand I jerked it vigorously.

I soon was awarded with the pleasurable hardening of the gristly shaft. His thing actually became stiff! Thinking that I could put it into my box I tried to hurry my coozie over to it, but no sooner had I done this and his tool became limp again.

"No, no, dear Flossie, it will not do those things anymore; it will stand no longer. You have to rub it and jerk it to make it feel good."

I felt so sorry for him that I put my arms around his neck and kissed him with my tongue. I began to once more manipulate his balls and prick. He, meanwhile, was running his fingers and hands around my ass, in my twat; he also kept his tongue busy either sucking my nipples, licking my belly or swabbing my asshole and twat.

"Flossie, you have a most wonderful tight pussy—oh, if only I had the power to use it I would gladly give up two years of my life! If I could only fuck!" He sighed and continued with his toils.

His staff was getting rigid again and my hand was moving up and down at a terrific pace. He grunted in explanation of his pleasure. I couldn't understand what kind of joy he was getting. Wasn't he past the age of feeling?

"Praised be Allah! It feels good all over . . . nice and warm . . . ravishing!" He wiggled and sputtered as he squeezed my titties and sucked my pussy; he also continued churning his finger in my asshole.

I was enjoying it all. I couldn't be so particular because I was hot for any kind of cunt stimulation that day. I felt a certain type of contentment because I was benefitting this old man. He seldom enjoyed a body so young and fresh as mine.

To my surprise his knob began to grow turgid as I began to spend. My erotic frenzy caused me to work on his joint even more nervously than I had been doing. The swelling continued and soon it began to bob. Nothing came out. His cries of appeased lust were most pleasing to hear. I never thought such was possible . . . it was, though! I came too, but I wanted more . . . so much more!

I arose and lay all over his body, trying to get his prick in. I was submerged in eroticism. I squeezed him and tried to swallow his limber prick in my hole ... failure greeted me. Finally I asked him to do something that would relieve my passions.

"Senator," I cried, "you have made me mad with a desire I cannot stand. Please, won't you do something for me! Here, kiss me here between my legs. Oh hurry!"

"Pet, I will do anything you say ... anything!" His crimson face beamed.

I settled on my hands and knees directly over his mouth. In this position I always enjoy a lap much better. My mouth was over his forlorn looking penis. I placed it in my mouth again. We began our respective labour. While he lashed his tongue in my ignited slit I swabbed my tongue around the head of his prick.

My feelings began to manifest themselves in spasms of exquisite sensations ... so very enhancing! So unreasonably wonderful! I do so dearly love the thrill of a man's tongue in my cunnie ... it is so nice and raspy.

I unconsciously buried my teeth in his still soft instruments. I began to feel it hardening once more! I wanted to see what it would feel like to have it climax in my mouth. In my ecstatic fury I laboured like a stalwart Trojan, so did he.

His body relaxed as I rolled off him. I

spent furiously. John lay as if he were dead; his eyes rolled deliriously.

When he came to and gathered enough aplomb he spoke: "Heavens, pet, you were extraordinary, making me come twice. Why, that's something I haven't done in years! I could marry a girl like you. I know you wouldn't have me."

"Senator, I do feel sorry for you, very sorry indeed, but I must have youth, fiery passions, and that you have not."

He arose, arranged his clothes and staggered out after thanking me a thousand times for the pleasures that I imparted to him. I also dressed and returned to our umbrella, Carl was still absent. I felt very much relieved.

It might appeal to some women to indulge with a man over fifty but as for me I shall always want a man whose vital parts are burning vigorously with passions, one whose organ rises to stateliness when it is touched or in the vicinity of a sensuous girl. Always a tool with a handsome pair of rock-hard balls—yes, that's my perfect sexual dish!

I am not trying to infer that I did not enjoy this experience. I shall always enjoy any type of stimulation pertaining to the sexual organs. This last one was a highly diversified incident, something that most women overlook. One's sensual experiences are never complete until one tries every cunt titillation that is known and strives to invent others.

The day that the jazzing vaudeville and show arrived finally dawned. I was nervous as the light crept into my room. I had lain awake most of the night trying to imagine how the next day would sum up. I had prophesied that this show would be my cure-all. It would be a definite means to an end, an end to Carl's chastity, an end to my suffering for his physical and mental love, an end to my cunt's sufferings for his gorgeous dick. I hoped all this and more. I even prayed that this should be so. Were my prayers to be answered. Only that day could answer this question. Can one blame me for my being nervous?

When Carl seated himself at the opposite end of the breakfast table he too appeared as though he hadn't slept. His eyes were bloodshot and his manners restless. I seldom showed it upon my face when I missed a night of sleep.

"Looks like you just came off of a drunk, Carl, didn't you sleep last night?"

"No, not very much."

"What is she a blonde or brunette?"

"You know me better, Floss. I have a hard time liking you, let alone strangers."

"That's encouraging. What did you dream about us?"

"It was not about us, it was more of a nightmare."

"What was it about? Eat! You haven't touched your food. Are you sick?"

"I'm not ill. I've got a funny, uncertain feeling."

"Now what do you mean? Why are you so mysterious?"

"I don't think I should tell you. Aw, it's too morbid. It's about that damned dream I had."

"You've got to tell me! Anyhow you'll probably forget about it at the show tonight, everybody in town is raving about it." That was a deliberate lie. I just said this so that I would appear to be an innocent victim of propaganda.

"Here's the story: I dreamed that dad came here riding in a coffin. Ordinarily I would think nothing of it but I reminded myself that he has not written since last week when he mentioned that he would join us here today, remember?"

"Yes, but why are you so upset about your dreams? Everybody dreams. It might have been something you ate?"

"The point is, why hasn't dad sent us some kind of a letter telling us exactly what day he'll be in. It's not like dad."

"Carl, didn't dad ever surprise you?"

"Sometimes. In a case of this kind he would not keep me in suspense about his health."

"Maybe he doesn't think that it is necessary. It's only a minor throat operation."

"Floss, I wish to God I could be swayed by you. Everything you say seems more reasonable than what I'm thinking but I just can't help myself."

"It will wear off as the day gets older." And then to myself I hoped it would because if it didn't he would be in no mood to go to the show. I needed him in a jovial frame of mind. The only thing that would lead to the success of my plans would be for Carl to receive a message from his parent. I wholeheartedly wished that it would state that he would be delayed for another week on account of business.

The day was a muggy one. It was misererable for Carl, because he desired some kind of news and for myself because I could not wait until we reached the show. I was determined to drag Carl there if those measures were necessary.

"How do you feel now, Carl?" I asked tenderly, as we tried to force ourselves to eat supper.

"I've felt bluer, I don't remember when though." He bravely forced a smile.

"What do you say? Let's take in the show. I don't feel so well myself. We can both stand a little diversion."

"And excitement," he added as though he was praying for a complete change of life.

We both began to dress for the occasion. I was in the midst of making my toilette when the bell rang. Maybelle left me to open the door but hearing Carl's voice already talking to the visitor she returned.

"Who was it, Maybelle, did you notice?"

"Just zee bell boy—you know zee one zat I ees fuckeeng regular."

"I thought you told me he has a small prick and that you weren't going to do it to him any more."

"He ees got such a sweet one I cannot help myself. He has learn me many new theengs that I weell show you een zee proper time."

"I have to look my best tonight, remember what I am going to try to do—either tonight or never! Maybelle, I've been dreaming since last night about it. I am terribly hot."

"I weel geeve your cunt a bath weeth my tongue before you leave. I know eet ees terribly een need of eet."

I laid over on the bed and let her go to work on me. I soon donated her another crop of my dew and then finished dressing.

I went into the living room to wait for Carl. He was not dressed yet, or if he was he might have stepped out for a few minutes. I sat there basking in a world of dreams, dreams of Carl's prick and my cunnie in every known embrace. I thought of every possible situation that might arise tonight and how I could conquer each one with tact. I wondered what Carl's reaction would be to the fucking scene. What could he think? I even took a silent vow that I would never covet another prick if I was promised his forever.

Marriage was out of the question. How could I marry the son of a man to whom I had been a mistress? That, his father would not sanction. And even if he did, sooner or later Carl would discover his father's and my relationship. But still the one thought that trickled through my mind, first like a small stream, then into the proportions of a mighty river—marriage was the surest outlet. It was the only cove in which I could find his presence and tool for life.

I then traced my movements in Carl's presence ever since I had known him. I tried to determine exactly whether he could look upon me with an eye for more than merely brotherly love. As far as I could remember our conversations were all warm and congenial, never a cross word. Of late he had shown a growing interest in me. He seemed to remember those little courtesies that so strongly appeal to the female's vanity. He catered to my comfort and assisted me with little tasks.

There is a certain attitude of unconcern and nonchalance that exists between brother and sister, a habit of assuming each other's existence, a mode of cohabitation where neither one cares about the other's affairs. As a rule brothers and sisters do not try to cultivate a more pleasant rapport among themselves. Each tries to surpass the other for family leadership, each demands the other to submit to his selfish motives. There was no semblance of any of these conditions between Carl and myself. We never had a quarrel. Kindness was the only emotion that existed, although I shed an emotion much stronger than all the many other ones combined . . . love, a deep, sincere, soul-fathoming passion.

I suddenly awoke from my waking, dreamy state. I thought I heard Carl approaching. It was only my maid with a corsage that she had forgotten to give me.

"How soon will Carl be ready?" I asked her.

"He ees not een hees room. I guess he step out for a few meenutes."

I looked about the floor and ceiling impatiently. I saw an envelope that had apparently dropped out of Carl's pocket lying in the centre of the room. I felt too lazy to get up and pick it up, but I couldn't keep my attention from straying upon it. My curiosity mounted. I just had to know what was in it! The battle between my curiosity and my desire to rest in my comfortable position raged for a few moments. Finally I collected enough energy to get up to pick up the message.

I looked at the envelope carefully, turning it over and over. It was from a local telegraph company, addressed to Carl. I didn't think that it was proper for me to read it, so I placed it on the table.

I reclined on the divan again to resume my wait for Carl. My mind somehow turned to the envelope on the table. A thought shot through my brain! Could it be possible? I sprang up and dashed over to the table nervously!

I had thought that this wire might have been the cause of Carl's disappearance. I didn't try to imagine its contents. I almost knew it was a message from his parent, telling him when he was to arrive.

I fingered it nervously, afraid to open it. I knew that if his dad were coming in, the show and the possible jazzing sequence to the show would be another miscarried dream. I perused it. His dad *was* indeed coming home. In a coffin.

10

10

Six months had passed since Roland died. Carl was more deeply touched than I. The clouds of melancholy were beginning to clear from our domicile.

During these six months we had travelled to all parts of the world to help Carl forget—at my suggestion. In his life I tried to play role of sister, mother and sweetheart. He may have never realized the latter; if he did he said nothing about it. In the evenings, after his return from the office, I would take his head, and lay it on my throbbing bosom and run my fingers soothingly through his hair. This was a practice that was only about two months old. He seemed to enjoy it immensely, like a child being petted by a tender and loving mother.

The present found us in New York. Roland had left his immense business interests to Carl. Apparently he had not thought death was near; I am most certain if he had he would have revised his will. Carl was now the captain of his parent's huge shipbuilding organization and, in order to be at the helm, it was necessary to live in New York.

I had visited Aunt Stella who, to my surprise, was married to a man of means. Her advice to me was: "There is nothing like it." Maybe that was the difference between infatuation; which was my illness with Don; animal love, which was the band that tied me to Roland; and love, which now firmly sewed me to Carl. Only with Carl did I feel that I could share my life, alone or otherwise. Only the future could tell.

Carl arrived home much later and apparently more fatigued than usual. We ate supper and then, as it was our custom, retired to the library, our most comfortable room.

"Carl, what was the trouble today? You look worried."

"I had the books audited and our cash shows two hundred and fifty thousand dollars more than the books."

"You should be happy," I moved towards him; we were both seated at opposite ends of a luxurious divan.

"Floss, I should. I don't know what I want. There seems to be something lacking in my life."

"There is," I said as I stroked his hair, "Something, Carl, that you should guess."

He seemed to think for a few moments, then he ceased as if he formed a silent conclusion. I wondered what this conclusion was. Was it the same I had in mind? He needed not only the soul of a woman but also her body. Did he guess what I meant?

We sat for about a half an hour in this comfortable silence, it was so comforting to be near Carl. I played with his hair and toyed with his tie until he was lulled into a near state of hypnosis. Involuntarily his arms found a resting place around my neck. He had never done this before.

I looked at him ... his eyes could not meet mine. Maybe he was ashamed of what he was doing. A will stronger than his guided his arms. His eyelids seemed to be weighted down by leaden lashes.

He drew me closer to him, slowly, steadily, with much tenderness. The silence was interrupted only by our breathing. There was a noticeable labour in Carl's efforts to obtain breath.

I was so completely puzzled that my mind ceased to function logically. What could he mean by taking me around? Did I hypnotize him into doing this? Was it mental telepathy? Or could he no longer obey his desire to resist me?

The feel of his warm, youthful, muscular body close to mine caused me to begin to wilt. My passions were being quickly aroused. Was this going to be the moment that I had been longing for ever since I had first met him? My intuition strived to answer the question. Fear that it would be wrong prevented it.

A moment later he crushed me to his chest, and when my nipples caressed his heaving breast, a dreamy, soothing, comfortable warmth circulated through me, a warmth that no other man had instilled. It was so comforting. I could have remained that way for hours and hours. It didn't cause me to sense a vulgar lust, but a clean, wholesome, unselfish eagerness to dip our bodies in the fusion pot of souls and have them moulded into one.

His clean, untarnished lips found mine. They met in such a sweet loving embrace; the kind that was a true edification to the purity of love. He wiped the corners of my lips with his moistened one, so fondly and so artfully. I felt so eased, yet a restlessness was rising within me, a restlessness that was caused by my want for greater contact.

Carl was already labouring to prevent a free emotional outburst—a tear or two rolled down his cheek. His inward self was crying, crying from a happiness that only the man in love can sense. Crying also for its genuine need for me. His glassy eyes spoke the strength of his emotions. His heavy breathing confirmed the telltale eyes' story.

I too was crying, perhaps for the same reasons he was, but I had others also. I was afraid to be happy—that is, too happy. I did not know how this would end I didn't care so very much so long as I was in his arms. I would never let him go.

"Carl, Carl, don't ever leave me." I sobbed very softly, as though afraid of losing him.

He did not reply but kissed me with greater burning enthusiasm and clutched my limp, submissive body more tightly. We were now lying down on the divan, stretched out full length, lips to lips, breast to chest, stomach to stomach, and his dove of love, enlarged and beating madly, pressed firmly against my pubic crop.

My heart felt heavy in spite of its wild pounding. My bones began to burn. The marrow seemed to melt—melt, and run into his. His heart felt like my heart. And I suppose the feelings were a mutual sensation.

I whispered softly, "Carl, Carl." What I meant by it I do not know. I was more deluged in delirium than I was sober. I could feel tornado-like waves of emotions sweeping through the caverns of my body, ready to remove me to insanity. I could feel my body begin to tremble convulsively. Carl's did likewise. We did not have to speak—we grasped each other's feelings.

Everything in the world suddenly became beautiful, picturesque. Everything was beginning to change to gold, sparkling diamonds, and to the glorious beatitude of the temples and bejewelled cities of the ancient Incas.

All this is the true emblem of love. A world that was formerly obscene becomes scenic. Sin becomes virtue, ugliness is transformed to sublimity, sadness changes to happiness, lust is no longer known. Such is love!

Slowly Carl lifted my skirt. Even this had a different feeling. A priceless act was to be performed! I did not help him. I let him find his way.

The crotch between my legs was drenched, drenched as it was never before. I sensed what I was about to undergo. In my delirium I half believed it. I felt many shocking pains shake my body, but they were such pleasurable pains. His lips were still relentlessly smothering mine. Our eyes were closed under the spell of a visionary blissfulness. Carl continued to lift my dress as best he could.

I could not resist the lure to press my stomach as mightily as I could to his, nor could I resist the temptation of pressing my Mons Veneris firmly to his scorching penis and then circling my bottom nervously. I was stark mad for the completion to this act. My sobs were hardly audible:

"Carl, dearest Carl, my boy. I am suffering so. I can see you are too." He opened his eyes and looked at mine, his head moved weakly, his eyes were filmy, he looked lost—so lost—a soul looking for its mate.

I rolled over on my back and he lay on top of me, with all his body excepting his legs. As though an unseen thread was pulling them apart, my legs opened, slowly, rhythmically, mechanically. He raised my dress further until my lacy pink panties were fully uncovered. He began to pull them down as best he could. I raised my bottom up to assist him. I could hardly find the reserve that was necesssary to use in order to remain sane.

As one hand crept around my bottom to denude my lower parts the other was drawn to my breasts, plucking, rubbing and soothing them to more intensely enrage my passions. Only once did he interrupt a kiss, and that was because he was losing control.

My legs were now spread as widely as they would go. Oh, how many months had I hankered for this moment to arrive? How I had dreamed and suffered and schemed to bring on this scene. Carl wormed between my legs with skill and care. Slowly he brought his thing to the opening of my torrid crevice. I had never been more anxious for a jazz, yet I had never used less initiative.

Carl had completely removed my panties, but he never looked to see how my denuded organ looked. I can assure you though, that it was crimson, puffed and anxious. Oh, would this promised-to-be heavenly act get under way? I could hardly extend my patience.

251

His tremendous tool found its way into my meshy, beating clefts. It was so hot that it almost singed my hairs. I spent in a glorious spasm, that's how powerful its radiation was. Its head was so mighty—could I insert it in my small, flaring hole? Oh I was so scared, I felt that I could!

"Carl, I love you," I moaned softly as I finished my first spend.

His tool found the opening to the aperture of my soul. Slowly it spread my tube. Gosh the pain was intense! I love it so! Then my hand went down to help guide it in. I caught a peep at it. I almost fainted! It was larger now than ever before. It was stretching me to the last stitch. But how incomparably good it was! After toiling for several minutes we managed to steer it in to its full eleven inches. Then an elaborate sacrifice to the god Eros began.

So vast is the difference of the sensation that one feels who has the huge prick of a loved one in them. There was nothing like it. I heaved my bottom around with mercuric speed, while he slowly and tenderly moved his loving tool in and out.

Not once did he remove his lips from mine during this celestial feast. His powerful love invigorator made the joy mount beyond recounting. My joints creaked under the terrific strain; my flesh was being eaten by a goodly feeling—pleasures, throbs, pains, oh every sensation that composes the recipe of eroticism was greatly exaggerated.

I cast my legs around his back. I was coming with Carl! His head began to swell—swell lovingly! The throbbings in my pussy grew to such proportions! only one gigantic feeling existed within me, a mammoth throbbing-itching! There was more bliss in this one jazz than all those I have had before, more joy, more feeling— love is that way!

Carl and I came at the same time. Other men's comes were merely jets—his was a hot steaming gusher. How wonderful it was to feel his hot lava-like liquids splashing against my uterus walls.

My tube clamped itself around his sporting jock with the tightness of a lover's hug. I felt so exhausted and weak from the intense excitement—very, very passive. I swooned during the blissful ecstasy of the die-away.

When I came to I began to sob hysterically. Nothing could pacify me. I was so very happy that I could not cease my crying. After months of careful planning I had finally won one round of my battle. There were many more to go.

When I revived, Carl was softly stroking my forehead. He too had tears in his eyes.

"Floss, forgive me," he said in a crying, hoarse whisper; "I couldn't help myself."

"Carl, I know we shouldn't—it's partly

my fault." I looked up at him through glassy eyes.

"Floss . . . you know . . .' he hesitated for a moment, "you know, Floss, you made me realize something tonight."

"You did too."

"Floss, I know now why I always felt something lacking.

He looked down at me, kissed me lightly on the forehead, ran his fingers through my hair. I reached for him with my arms, drew his head down on my chest and let it sink in the spongy softness.

At last he raised his head, looked into my eyes solemnly and whispered:

"Floss . . . I love you. I just realised I can't get along without you. I don't ever want to lose you. Will you marry me?"

I was so overcome by joy that I could only hug and kiss him—an emblematic answer.

STAR BOOKS ADULT READS

FICTION

BEATRICE	Anonymous	£2.25*
EVELINE	Anonymous	£2.25*
MORE EVELINE	Anonymous	£2.25*
FRANK & I	Anonymous	£2.25*
A MAN WITH A MAID	Anonymous	£2.25*
A MAN WITH A MAID 2	Anonymous	£2.25*
A MAN WITH A MAID 3	Anonymous	£2.25*
OH WICKED COUNTRY	Anonymous	£2.25*
ROMANCE OF LUST VOL 1	Anonymous	£2.25*
ROMANCE OF LUST VOL 2	Anonymous	£2.25*
SURBURBAN SOULS VOL 1	Anonymous	£2.25*
SURBURBAN SOULS VOL 2	Anonymous	£2.25*
DELTA OF VENUS	Anais Nin	£1.60*
LITTLE BIRDS	Anais Nin	£1.60*
PLAISIR D'AMOUR	A.M.Villefranche	£2.25
JOIE D'AMOUR	A.M.Villefranche	£2.25

STAR Books are obtainable from many booksellers and newsagents. If you have any difficulty tick the titles you want and fill in the form below.

Name _____

Address _____

_____

Send to: Star Books Cash Sales, P.O. Box 11, Falmouth, Cornwall, TR10 9EN.

Please send a cheque or postal order to the value of the cover price plus:
UK: 55p for the first book, 22p for the second book and 14p for each additional book ordered to the maximum charge of £1.75.

BFPO and EIRE: 55p for the first book, 22p for the second book, 14p per copy for the next 7 books, thereafter 8p per book.

OVERSEAS: £1.00 for the first book and 25p per copy for each additional book.

While every effort is made to keep prices low, it is sometimes necessary to increase prices at short notice. Star Books reserve the right to show new retail prices on covers which may differ from those advertised in the text or elsewhere.

*NOT FOR SALE IN CANADA

STAR BOOKS ADULT READS

FICTION

ADVENTURES OF A SCHOOLBOY	Anonymous	£2.25
AUTOBIOGRAPHY OF A FLEA	Anonymous	£2.25*
MEMOIRES OF DOLLY MORTEN	Anonymous	£2.25
LAURA MIDDLETON	Anonymous	£2.25
THREE TIMES A WOMAN	Anonymous	£2.25*
THE BOUDOIR	Anonymous	£2.25*
THE LUSTFUL TURK	Anonymous	£2.25*
MAUDIE	Anonymous	£2.25*
RANDIANA	Anonymous	£2.25*
ROSA FIELDING	Anonymous	£2.25*
JOY	Joy Laurey	£2.25
JOY AND JOAN	Joy Laurey	£2.25
INSTRUMENT OF PLEASURE	Celeste Piano	£2.25
OPUS PISTORUM	Henry Miller	£2.25*

STAR Books are obtainable from many booksellers and newsagents. If you have any difficulty tick the titles you want and fill in the form below.

Name _____

Address _____

_____

Send to: Star Books Cash Sales, P.O. Box 11, Falmouth, Cornwall, TR10 9EN.

Please send a cheque or postal order to the value of the cover price plus: UK: 55p for the first book, 22p for the second book and 14p for each additional book ordered to the maximum charge of £1.75.

BFPO and EIRE: 55p for the first book, 22p for the second book, 14p per copy for the next 7 books, thereafter 8p per book.

OVERSEAS: £1.00 for the first book and 25p per copy for each additional book.

While every effort is made to keep prices low, it is sometimes necessary to increase prices at short notice. Star Books reserve the right to show new retail prices on covers which may differ from those advertised in the text or elsewhere.

*NOT FOR SALE IN CANADA